ZANE PRESENTS

Loyalty

AMONG FRIENDS

Dear Reader:

What if you found yourself in this position: one of your friends is cheating with another friend's husband. Some of you might tell the married friend, but how difficult would that be? Or perhaps you would confront the husband and not discuss with either friend.

In *Loyalty Among Friends*, Pat Tucker and Earl Sewell, in their second coauthored title, deal with this controversial situation with Ava, who finds herself in the middle of the lives of two friends.

I'm sure you will enjoy the journey of this dramatic tale of infidelity, lust and trust between the married Ava; Bailey, the sexy flirt; and Jayden and Sylvia, the married couple. See how this entangled web plays out in this state of affairs that puts friendships to an ultimate test.

Check out the authors' first project, *A Social Affair*, which highlights the world of online cheating.

As always, I appreciate the love and support shown to Strebor Books, myself, and our efforts to bring you cutting-edge stories.

Blessings,

Zane

Publisher
Strebor Books
www.simonandschuster.com

ZANE PRESENTS

Loyalty

AMONG FRIENDS

A NOVEL BY

PAT TUCKER &
EARL SEWELL

SBI

STREBOR BOOKS

NEW YORK LONDON TORONTO SYDNEY

Strebor Books
P.O. Box 6505
Largo, MD 20792
http://www.streborbooks.com

ISBN 978-1-59309-530-7
ISBN 978-1-4767-4678-4 (ebook)
LCCN 2014935328

First Strebor Books trade paperback edition September 2014

Cover design: www.mariondesigns.com
Cover photograph: © Keith Saunders/Marion Designs

10 9 8 7 6 5 4 3 2 1

Manufactured in the United States of America

For information regarding special discounts for bulk purchases, please contact Simon & Schuster Special Sales at 1-866-506-1949 or business@simonandschuster.com

The Simon & Schuster Speakers Bureau can bring authors to your live event. For more information or to book an event, contact the Simon & Schuster Speakers Bureau at 1-866-248-3049 or visit our website at www.simonspeakers.com.

CHAPTER ONE

Bailey

When I finally came up for air and seductively crawled up the length of Richard's lean, naked body, I could feel the heat rise, among other things. With his essence still on my lips, I was ready for him to reciprocate the pleasure I had just delivered.

"Daayum, that was good," he managed.

His voice was shaky, and he was still breathing hard like he had trouble catching his breath. I beamed with pride. If I didn't know anything else, I knew how to please a man. He rubbed my breasts as I rolled over to his side of the bed, and tried to adjust my body next to his.

"Whheew, girl! It's been a while since I had some expert head like that. That was good!"

You're damn right, it was good. I have the aching jaws to prove it.

"I'm glad you enjoyed it, daddy; now it's my turn," I cooed.

Usually, I didn't like playing tit-for-tat like that, but this one seemed a little slow. His body was nice, but he was a lazy lover, and who had time for that? I didn't have any problems letting a man know exactly what I wanted.

Suddenly, Richard rose and sat upright. He swung his long legs over the edge of the bed and onto the floor. I lay there confused, wondering whether he needed some water or something before round two.

He looked over his shoulder at me. "Uhh, what's your name again?"

I began to fume. "Bailey. You know, like the liquor." I didn't even try to hide the sarcasm in my tone.

"Oh, yeah, that's easy enough to remember. Well, uhh, look here, Bailey, I got an early meeting tomorrow morning," he said. Then, he yawned.

I drew my eyebrows together. "Are you serious right now?"

"Oh, nah, nah. It ain't nothing like that. I mean, it was real nice meeting you, but like I said, I gotta get up real early in the morning."

It was my turn to pop up in bed like a jack-in-the-box. The heat that crawled up my naked back threatened to sear my hairline. My neck started twisting before I could get my words out good. "You've got to be kidding, right?" I hissed.

"See, Hailey. Now, calm down. It's not like that. It's not what you think."

I got up from his bed, and stormed around his junky room, picking up my clothes. *What man in his right mind brings a woman home to this pigsty?*

"It's Bailey!" I snarled, as I snatched my bra off of the old-fashioned lamp shade and put it back on.

"Oh, my bad, my bad. Yeah, that's right. Bailey, like the liquor, right?"

If looks could kill, Richard would've been a corpse. Once I was dressed, he grabbed a robe and got up to follow me to the front door.

"Shit, where's my purse?" I looked around his crowded living room, frustrated. I really need to be more selective.

He glanced around the dark room, like he was trying to be

helpful. I wanted to knee him in his groin, to take away some of the bliss I had blessed him with earlier.

"Hey, I'ma call you," he lied.

I grabbed my purse from his coffee table and rolled my eyes.

He opened the door and waited.

Before I stepped out, I looked at him and said, "Save the bull; you don't even have my number, remember? I followed you from the club and we were gonna exchange numbers once we got here."

"Oh, yeah. My bad."

When the fool yawned again, I shook my head.

"Later. Hope you're late for your meeting," I said, as I walked out.

"Oh yeah, thanks," the idiot responded.

I felt like crap as I walked down the long hallway from his apartment and got on the elevator. There had to be a better way. I was sick and tired of meeting losers and falling for their lame lines and excuses. At the club, good ol' Richard was all gung-ho about hooking up, and us having a possible future together.

He had filled my head with so much bull that he had me thinking we might actually make it to the altar. I knew I had just met him hours earlier, but he'd fed me so many lines about being tired of the dating scene, I thought he might be different. He'd said he was ready to leave the clubs and slow down. I could relate to everything he'd said. I felt the same way.

I wasn't trying to screw him the very first night we met, but I thought we had mad chemistry. I agreed with him that we needed to get to know each other better in a quieter place. At the time, it made sense since his apartment wasn't far from the historic Gaslamp Quarter in downtown San Diego.

Besides, he had already told me his intentions, and I felt like I needed to take a chance if I ever wanted to find true love.

As I drove home, I couldn't help but beat myself up. I was successful in every other aspect of my life. I was college educated with a MBA, worked in commercial real estate, and took very good care of my body. I didn't understand why I couldn't find a man. Scratch that. Bump a man. I wanted a husband!

Hell, I had no problems finding men. They were drawn to me like flies to shit! Unfortunately, I couldn't seem to hang on to a decent one to save my life.

Thank God I had enough sense not to tell Richard that I lived close by too. I lived at one of San Diego's trendiest addresses. The Alta was a soaring twenty-one-story building with designer stores, cafes, and restaurants. The mixed-use building also had a combination of trendy lofts, condos, and penthouses. Every day, I walked into spectacular views of the scenic San Diego Bay, and at night, it was sparkling city lights.

My two-bedroom condo had everything—dramatic, vaulted ceilings, tons of window walls that allowed natural light to pour into every corner of the space, and a large, private terrace. The only thing missing was my Mr. Right.

After I pulled into the underground parking garage, I got out of my car and tried to push thoughts of my horrible night aside.

"I'm done with the losers in the club. I mean it!" I muttered as I rode the elevator up to my place. I was physically and emotionally exhausted.

The sun was coming up by the time I showered and changed for bed. As I lay in my massive, four-poster, king-sized bed unable to sleep, I considered taking an Ambien. I quickly decided against it, since I was meeting my best friend, Ava, for brunch and I didn't want to oversleep.

Suddenly, thoughts of whether I'd share my story with her crowded my mind. Ava and I had been friends since the second grade. But our lives had taken such different paths that sometimes I put distance between us on purpose.

I loved Ava like the sister I never had, but the truth was, I looked better than her. I was more successful, yet she was happily married, and I was still miserably single. It just didn't make sense.

Over the last five years, we'd grown closer and I was happy about that. I told myself it wasn't Ava's fault I couldn't find a husband. It sure wasn't for a lack of trying. Both Ava and her husband, Isaac, had tried to fix me up several times, but nothing ever stuck.

I decided I'd tell her about what had happened last night, but I'd give her the abbreviated version. *What in the hell was so wrong with me?* In the darkness, I lay wide awake, staring up at the ceiling.

"Dear God, why did you make me so beautiful, yet unlovable?"

CHAPTER TWO

Ava

"Iiiisac!" I screamed.

My husband worked my last nerve with his hour-long showers. What in God's name was he doing in there? I hated to burst in on him. I knew he'd want some sex, and I wasn't in the mood. But his irritating mama had already called three times, and she refused to hang up.

"Mrs. Goodson, can't I get him to call you back when he gets out? I guess he can't hear me," I said into the phone.

"I'ma wait for you to go get him. I ain't got all mornin' to be waitin' on Isaac's call. I got thangs to do," she replied.

"Yes, ma'am," I sighed and got up from my nice, comfortable bed. I padded over to the bathroom in our master suite and knocked on the door. "Honey, your mom is holding on the phone."

"Tell her I'll call right back!"

"Not gonna work. She's called three times already."

I twisted the handle and walked into the steam-filled bathroom. It smelled so good in there. I loved the scent of my husband's body wash, and scolded myself for not wanting to join him in the shower.

He opened the shower door and walked out dripping wet. After he took the phone, he reached over and tapped me on my behind.

"Quit," I said.

"You know you like it."

Isaac's body couldn't qualify him for any athletic teams. He had a little too much around the middle, and a budding beer belly. But I loved every inch of him.

His last physical wasn't the best, and the doctor told me I needed to change both of our diets. I was trying, but it wasn't easy. We both loved my Southern cooking.

My husband's abdomen may not have been able to compete with any six packs, but he was a good, handsome man with a kind heart. When he started balding in his late twenties, I told him to shave his head. That had been his signature look long before it became the most popular style for black men.

Isaac was about five feet ten inches tall, with copper-colored skin. He had broad shoulders and a square face.

"Hey, Mama," I heard him say into the phone as I left the bathroom.

There was no point in going back to bed. I had a brunch date in a couple of hours. I went into the kitchen to start coffee, and tried to figure out what to fix for Isaac. Truth be told, I probably didn't need to be brunching at all. I had picked up a good twenty-five pounds, and couldn't lose them with all the cooking I did.

Luckily for me, Isaac didn't seem to mind.

"I love me a woman with curves," he'd say. If he liked anything else, it wouldn't matter. We'd been married for nearly twenty-two years, and neither of us planned to go anywhere. I fixed Isaac an egg and avocado breakfast sandwich and got ready for my brunch date.

I was meeting Bailey at the Grant Grill. It was closer to her, so I figured she'd probably beat me there. I thought about Isaac and his complaint about his food before I left.

"Hey, where's the meat?" he'd asked after he bit into the sandwich.

"Doctor said to lay off the sodium." I'd grabbed my bag and kissed him on his forehead.

"Humph, well what you 'bout to go eat?"

"Brunch food."

"Bring me back a doggie bag," he said.

Minutes later, I parked, rushed into the restaurant, and scanned the room searching for Bailey.

"How many?" the hostess asked.

"Oh, I'm meeting a friend here; not sure if she's here yet," I said.

"Would you like to go take a look?"

Just as I was about to walk all the way into the restaurant, Bailey's high-pitched voice startled me.

"Ava Goodson, get over here and give me some love, girl!" Bailey rushed over, threw her arms around me, and squeezed. She pulled back to give me a dramatic, signature air kiss to each cheek. "I'm so glad you finally made it."

I knew I was late, but I didn't think I was *that* late.

"You look good, Bailey." And she did. The male eyes that followed her every step were proof of that. Everything about Bailey was loud and designed to grab attention.

"You ladies ready?" the hostess asked.

"Yes," I answered. We followed her to a table.

Heads turned and eyes gawked as Bailey sashayed in all her designer-infused glory. I wasn't sure whether it was her gray contact lenses, fake lashes, or her figure-hugging wrap dress that did it. But Bailey was known for her attention-grabbing outfits.

When she'd invited me to brunch, I thought relaxed, casual, and comfortable attire would do. I should've known better. Compared to her, I might as well have been wearing a dusty, old potato sack.

My jeans and Jones New York blouse made me look more like her assistant than her girlfriend.

Once seated, Bailey looked around the room and gave her admirers one last smile. She saved the dramatic frown for me.

"Oh my God, Ava! Wait 'til I tell you about my horrible date last night." Her expression deadpanned.

I swear a few heads snapped in our direction. The hungry expressions on the men's faces all but begged her to give them the chance to make it up to her.

"Date?" I was confused. "I thought you said you were going to the club last night."

I knew good and well that if Bailey had a date, we would've been on the phone analyzing everything down to the matching bra and panty set she should wear. Something wasn't adding up, but I wasn't sure I was in the mood to do the math.

"Girl, I did. That's where we met, errr, I mean, agreed to meet," Bailey said.

I frowned.

"So, what did you expect? Who goes out on a date to a club, Bailey? Whose idea was that?"

Bailey rolled her eyes at the ceiling and gave me an exasperated look. "You are so lucky you have a husband. I'm telling you, these men out here..." Bailey scrunched up her nose. "There's nothing good available, believe me."

"Yeah, but, Bailey, you should never take a date to the club or let him take you to one for that matter."

"Well, when I agreed to go out with him, who knew he was talking about the club? Then, when we went back to his place, and he could barely keep his hands off me," she said. "It was awful!"

"If you guys went to the club, when did you go to his house?"

"Oh, sweet Jesus! Ava, girl! Don't look now, but he just walked in. And look at that Plain Jane he's got on his arm! Ugh! We need to go somewhere else. I've lost my appetite."

Panic settled in quickly. I didn't want to leave after the heavenly scent of fresh waffles had teased my senses. I didn't understand why we couldn't stay there, but the answer came quicker than I expected.

CHAPTER THREE

Jayden

The morning alarm on my cell gurgled like an old telephone. I opened my eyes, sat upright, and placed my bare feet on the carpeted floor beside the bed. I extended my arms high above my head, stretched, and yawned. Reaching over, I turned on the hotel lamp next to the bed. I glanced over my shoulder at my wife, Sylvia, who had on her black eye mask and ear plugs. She wasn't a morning person like me or our son, Greg, who was in an adjoining room. I knew that he was awake. I heard water from his bathroom as it rushed through a pipe in the wall. We had arrived in Seattle yesterday from San Diego where we lived. Greg and I had come to participate in a half marathon. I rose to my feet and while heading towards the bathroom, I listened to my toes pop like breakfast cereal drowning in a bowl of milk. *Aging is a bitch*, I thought as I entered the bathroom.

When I finished my ablutions, I came out and headed toward my running gear which I had laid out the night before. I put on my heart monitor, shorts, and running top with my bib number already attached. I threw a pair of light jogging pants and a matching long-sleeved shirt on top. I grabbed my hat, watch, keys, and duffle bag which were filled with other necessities. I lightly knocked on the door that connected my room with my son's. He opened it, and I stepped inside. I saw that he was already dressed.

"Hey, Dad. I just need to put on my shoes and I'll be ready to go."

"Take your time. There is no rush." I shoved my hands deep into the pockets of my jogging pants and waited.

"Where is Mom?" Greg sat at the foot of the bed to put on his running shoes.

"She's still asleep." I moved toward a window to take a peek outside.

"I thought she wanted to be there at the start of the race?"

I shrugged. "Your mother is notorious for saying one thing and doing another. You know that."

"You're right, but she said that she would watch our bags for us so that we wouldn't have to leave them in the tent area."

"Son, let me give you a bit of advice. It's something that I've learned over the twenty years I have been married to your mother. When she is asleep, don't wake her."

"Dad."

"What? It's the truth." I moved toward the door of his hotel room. Greg looked at the adjoining door, considering waking up his mother.

"I'm going to go let her know that we're leaving," he said.

"Suit yourself. I'll be in the car waiting."

A few minutes later, Greg exited the hotel and approached the car. He opened the door and got in.

"She's coming," he said as he settled into the back seat.

The thought of having to wait irritated me. I glanced at the clock. It was 4:45 a.m., and the race started in an hour.

"It's going to take her forever to get herself moving and get down here." I impatiently thumped the steering with my thumb.

"Why don't you like waiting for her?"

"It annoys me. I like showing up early, and your mother believes in being fashionably late. Thanks to her, we were late for your junior high and high school graduations."

"I remember that. You guys arrived after I had walked across the stage. That's just her way, Dad," Greg defended his mother.

"I swear, sometimes I believe your mother has some type of late gene in her DNA."

Greg sat silently, and I reclined my head against the headrest. Thirty minutes later, Sylvia came out of the hotel and got into the car.

"Okay, I'm ready, but you need to find a Starbucks or coffee shop where I can get a cup of coffee before we get to the race," she said.

"We don't have time to do that. You'll have to figure out where to get a cup once you're there." There was bitterness in my tone of voice as I backed up and sped off.

"Damn, slow down. You don't have any reason to be so wound up."

Greg spoke up from the backseat. "I didn't want to ask this, but are you guys going to be okay when I leave?"

"What do you mean, honey?" asked Sylvia.

"I mean are you guys cool with each other?"

"Of course we are, honey."

"Dad?" Greg wanted confirmation from me, but I remained quiet.

"Your father knows he's crazy about me, honey," Sylvia gave the response she believed was locked in my head. I glanced at her and thought about some of our wasted history. A hard line formed on her lips as she positioned her head against the headrest and closed her eyes. *There is an overdraft fee in my bank of tolerance for you*, I thought to myself as I headed toward our destination.

When we arrived, the race had begun. Greg and I had a limited amount of time to warm up before we stripped down to our running shorts and tank tops. We infused ourselves into the throngs of runners who steadily marched out onto the race course.

"Do you want to try to catch up to our pace group?" Greg asked as I adjusted my running cap.

"Yeah; come on." I picked up the pace. My son had started running with me when he was nine years old. He was a natural distance runner. He was tall and lean like me, and was in excellent shape. He had gone away to college on a running scholarship and had received his undergraduate degree in broadcast journalism. In a few days' time, Greg would leave home for good. He'd accepted a job offer for a position at a television station in Chicago.

"Come on, old man." Greg roused the competitor in me.

"Have I ever told you the story of the old and young bulls?" I asked as we snaked our way around slower runners.

"No."

"Well, there were these two bulls. One was young, and the other one was old. They were father and son. They were sitting on top of a hill looking down at a bunch of cows grazing in the pasture. The young bull turned to his father and said, 'Why don't we run down the hill and get one of those cows for ourselves?' The father laughed and said, 'Why don't we walk down the hill, and get them all?'"

"Ha, ha." Greg chuckled as we caught up to our pace group. We settled comfortably into our individual strides as we ran alongside each other.

"I'm proud of you, Greg," I said breathlessly as we continued along.

"I know, but don't get sentimental on me during this race."

"Who said I was getting sentimental? Saying that I'm proud of you is another way of saying, 'I can't wait for you to get the hell out of the house so that I can have my life back'." I laughed as we turned a corner and zoomed past mile one.

Greg and I continued to run side-by-side until mile eighteen, which was when he began to pull away from me. I still had enough strength and endurance left in my body to keep pace with him. *Not this time*, I thought to myself.

As he pulled ahead, in a metaphorical way, I was letting him go so that he could become his own man. I had kept him out of trouble and gotten him through college. He was a smart and ambitious young man with the challenges of life ahead of him. I would no longer be at his side the way I had been most of his life. He was now in full control of his own destiny.

The moment was a time of change for me as well. It was the dawn of another stage in my life. This time, I would work hard not to make foolish errors as I had done in my youth. I felt warm and bright, to the point of bursting, like the sun was rising from somewhere deep inside of me. I welcomed the feeling. I had been waiting on its arrival for a long time.

CHAPTER FOUR

Bailey

"Who's ready to make some money today?" My battle cry was always the same every morning as I strode into the office. With my heels *click-clacking* against the tiles, I was on a natural high after my high-powered workout. My loud and boisterous entrance always shattered the soft jazz that mingled with work chatter, ringing phones, and the constant buzz of office machines.

I had to bring an energetic vibe into the office. My team at Baccard Development, an international corporate real estate management firm, could get a little lax. And when we were lax, we didn't make money. I needed them to understand that every single day was high-stakes poker, and I only played to win.

"Your messages, Miss Jones." My assistant, Diane Brown, handed me a stack of slips. Diane, a fiftyish woman with a mane of sculpted, jet-black curls, refused to upgrade to the new digital message system. She was old school.

Over the years, I had earned Diane's respect, largely based on my performance. I brought in tons of business, and business meant money. She had the ear of owner, Barron Baccard, and I knew Diane's reports about me were favorable.

The building we were housed in was at eighty-nine percent

capacity, which was excellent in this economy. I was on the verge of bringing in a new anchor for the penthouse space. I was on fire when it came to work. I loved the corporate real estate environment, and was able to thrive because it was a male-dominated industry. I may not know how to keep a man, but I certainly knew how to make men money.

Once inside my office, I sat behind my massive glass desk, flipping through the messages Diane had given me. Seeing nothing pressing, I checked my calendar and noticed two meetings. Since both were scheduled for later in the afternoon, I got up to lock my office door.

"Diane, hold my calls for the next two hours, please; I have a video chat with our Belize offices."

She glanced up from her desk, her face lined with confusion as she looked at me. Diane liked to be on top of everything in the office. But there were times when I had to let her know who was really in charge. For the most part, we all worked well together and that's how we were able to be successful.

"It's a last-minute call that I personally scheduled," I told her.

"Oh, okay," she said curtly, nodded, then started to bang on her computer's keyboard.

Once I locked my door, I leaned against it, sighed hard, and tried to calm myself. I walked to my large windows and closed the blinds. I needed quiet time. I needed to focus. The mess that was yesterday's brunch still had me uneasy. My mind drifted back to that moment in the restaurant.

"Nooo! I said don't look!" I'd told Ava as we sat at our table. But of course it was too late. The minute the words fell from my lips, her head had snapped in his direction.

"Who?" Ava had asked.

I sighed hard and tried to lower my voice.

"That's the jerk I told you about from last night, Richard what's-his-name," I said through gritted teeth as I eyed him. "Oh my God! Would you look at her?"

"I can't take it. Either you want me to look or you don't!"

The moment Richard's eyes connected with mine, he stopped cold in his tracks. He stared like he had just seen a ghost. The librarian look-alike he was with stopped too, and followed his gaze to me. The woman's hands flew to her hefty hips, and her neck began to snake.

By now, they were inches from our table. The woman had the nerve to twist up her face at me, and then scream, "Is that the bitch's panties I found behind the pillow on your sofa?"

Oh no she didn't! Unable to control myself, I sprang from my chair. "Who you calling a bitch?"

The look on stupid Richard's face was pathetic. He glanced at me as if he was pleading with his eyes, then nervously back at his woman.

Suddenly, she used both hands and shoved him hard in the chest. "I'm so sick of this shit with you. I keep telling you to stop picking up these skeezers at the club, but you just can't stop!"

Gasps filled the air. Every eye focused on us. I was used to being the center of attention, but not like this. I was so pissed at Richard.

"Skeezer?" I belted out a laugh and started toward her.

Ava jumped up and blocked my path. "No, ma'am!" she whispered. "You said it yourself, he's not worth it."

Richard stumbled back, but caught his balance, and looked at me with sheer disgust. "She ain't nobody, Belinda. I picked her up in the club, and she all but begged to follow me home. But, babe, I didn't touch that bitch. I just let her suck me off."

I felt myself stiffen, as rage tore through every cell in my body. I was ready to kill. "You filthy, lying bastard!" I shrieked.

The woman looked me up and down, with a menacing glare.

"I don't even know her name. Tequila, or some mess like that. C'mon, babe, you know she ain't even my type," he cried. "Look at her!"

The woman snatched a glass off a nearby table, and doused Richard's face in ice water. He hollered like a banshee, and threw the entire restaurant into an uproar.

Other customers stopped to stare. They pointed, whispered, and took in the scene. The staff seemed unsure about what to do, and Ava looked mortified. I wasn't sure if it was what Richard was saying, or the big, nasty scene that unfolded in the middle of the trendy restaurant.

When my cell phone rang, I snapped out of the horrible memory, and glanced down at the caller ID. The word *Blocked* flashed across my screen.

It was the fourth time this caller had dialed my number. Instead of ignoring it again, I slid my finger across the screen and placed the phone to my ear to answer. "Bailey Jones."

"Bailey, I heard you got mad skills with them lips. I think I'm close to your office; I can come right over," the caller said.

"What the fu—" I swallowed the stinging reply that sat on the tip of my tongue, and ended the call.

"Yup, I really need to be more selective," I murmured aloud.

CHAPTER FIVE

Ava

Getting up out of bed when I felt like it was incredible. I played hooky from work today, so I wasn't on anybody's schedule or clock. Isaac was an engineer for the city, and had given me the option to quit my job a while back. I didn't mind working, but I enjoyed days like this.

My job at a construction company wasn't anything to brag about, but it helped pay the bills. I worked in Human Resources, alongside my best friend, Sylvia Henner, but I was mostly a paper pusher. Needless to say, I couldn't wait to get on the phone with Sylvia so I could fill her in on my eventful Sunday. She'd been gone all day yesterday to watch her husband and son compete in a marathon. She called me during her commute this morning, but Isaac went in late, so we weren't able to dish like I wanted.

After a light breakfast and a cup of coffee, I had to keep myself busy to stop from calling her. I looked around our meticulous home, but nothing was out of place. The contemporary décor was brimming with bright colors, golds, and various hues of blue. I walked into the formal living room and fluffed the bright turquoise pillows. They really popped against the dark-chocolate, leather sectional. I used the tip of my house shoe to smooth out the area rug and scanned the room again. Unable to find any busy work in there, I made my way back to the kitchen.

"Oooh, let me check in on Bailey," I said aloud. I hated to call her on the office phone. That damn Diane was worse than an FBI agent on assignment. She wanted to know who you were, why you were calling, whether your call was business or pleasure, your Social Security number, what and who you claimed on your taxes, and so on and so on. It was absolutely exhausting to talk to her. I pulled out my cell phone and hit the button to dial Bailey's.

"Hey, lady, how you feeling today?" I asked cheerfully.

When she sighed hard in my ear, I rolled my eyes. I didn't understand how she did it. Bailey's life was always completely drama filled. I had all but given up on trying to help the child find a man. I inhaled and braced myself for the latest episode of *As-Bailey's-World-Turns*.

I was the calm and laid-back type, but Bailey's zeal and wild ways made her the polar opposite. It never seemed to matter before since we mostly complemented each other. We got together once a week, or once every couple of weeks, to shoot the breeze, dish the dirt, or just to hang. Despite our stark differences, we'd been close for as long as I could remember.

"Girl, that fool Richard keeps playing on my phone," Bailey said.

"Playing on your phone?"

I couldn't believe Bailey's luck with men. It seemed as if she found one loser after another. I had run out of advice for her a very long time ago, and was simply hanging on for the ride. And with Bailey, that ride was anything but smooth.

"I was calling to make sure you were okay after the drama at brunch yesterday."

"Oh, girl, please! Of course I'm okay. Why wouldn't I be? I mean, it's very clear to me that Richard was trying to juggle two women at one time," she responded matter-of-factly.

I didn't want to burst Bailey's bubble, but that man had been pretty clear that they were not on a date like she had told me. According to him, he'd picked her up in the club, and took her back to his place. I hated when she felt she had to lie to me. I was never judgmental. She knew she had no business picking up men in bars and clubs. Who does that these days? I wondered why she wasn't scared of getting HIV or some other sexually transmitted disease. But I wouldn't dare ask.

Bailey carried on. "Yeah, I'm gonna have to call the cops if he doesn't quit."

"So that woman he was with, are they in a relationship?" I asked.

"Girl, I don't know. He'd been trying to get with me for so long, I finally decided to throw his homely behind a bone and that's how he acts?" Bailey huffed. "He's just mad I wouldn't give him a taste. I get so tired of these bums trying to act like they ain't got no damn common sense when I tell them I'm not feeling them."

"Is that what really happened, Bailey?" I couldn't take it anymore. "I mean, c'mon. Keep it real."

"Umm, what's that supposed to mean, Ava?" Her question was thick with sarcasm. I could picture the expression on her face, so I backed off.

I wasn't trying to fight with Bailey. I really was only calling to check up on her. After we were tossed out of Grant Grill, I wasn't sure I ever wanted to show my face downtown again.

"I'm just saying he was talking all crazy. But you know what? I could tell he was one of those men who'd probably say anything when he got caught red-handed."

"That's exactly what happened, girl! I'm telling you, if that chick knows like I know, she'd dump Richard's behind. He ain't nothing but a lying, dirty snake in the grass," Bailey said with mock authority.

When my other line clicked in my ear, I was relieved and happy to take the call.

"Hey, Bailey, that's my other line and I need to grab this. We'll catch up later, okay?"

"Go ahead, girl. I need to get ready for a meeting anyway. I'll talk to you later."

I quickly clicked over to the other line. "Sylvia! Girl! Do I have some hot drama to share with you." I hollered into the phone without as much as a hello.

"Dang, girl, lemme guess. It's that Bailey friend of yours, huh?"

"You know it is. Girl, wait 'til I tell you what happened at brunch yesterday." I howled.

"Oh, let me get up and close my door," Sylvia said excitedly. "This sounds like it's gonna be juicy!"

"You know what, I need to hang up and call you right back. I was just talking to her on the other line when you called in. You know how I am when I'm talking about folks; I don't need no party line tripping me up," I said.

We laughed.

"I feel you there. Call me right back!" Sylvia demanded.

CHAPTER SIX

Jayden

I had just picked up Bo, the family's brown-and-black German Shepherd, from a nearby dog hotel that took care of him while we were away. Bo had suckered me into bringing him home from the pet store three years ago. He'd duped me with his innocent eyes and playfulness. I had gone in to purchase a new fish tank and walked out with dog food and supplies, giving my word that I would be back for Bo.

"Sylvia, I'm home," I called out. When she did not respond, I decided to go through the house and search for her. She wasn't in the kitchen or den, so I headed upstairs. I noticed the bedroom door was closed, but I heard her laughing. I opened the door and found her comfortably resting on the chaise lounge sofa.

"I'm home."

Sylvia acknowledged me and then smeared away tears of laughter from her cheeks. She then waved me away so that she could continue talking.

I exited the bedroom, walked down to the end of the corridor, and opened the door to Greg's old bedroom. I stood in the center of the room and felt both pride and sadness as I thought about how my life had shifted into its empty nest phase. I heard Bo's paws clicking rhythmically against the wooden floor. I looked over my shoulder and saw his ears tucked back and his tail playing tennis as he approached. Bo sat down next to me and positioned his head under my left hand so that I could pet him.

"He's gone, Bo," I whispered. Bo whined. He sensed how I felt. When my sentimental feelings abated, I thought about how to repurpose the space. The first thing I wanted was to remove the bed and dresser and place them in the attic. Those items could remain there for a while in case Greg had to come home for one reason or another. I noticed that the carpet needed to be pulled up, and the walls in the room needed a fresh coat of paint. I moved toward his closet and opened it. The closet walls could use some paint too. Bo trotted into the closet and began sniffing around. He found a loose section of the carpet and began to paw at it.

"Bo. Leave it," I commanded. Bo turned around and walked out of the closet, but I noticed that he had actually found something. I pulled the overhead string to turn on the closet light and moved toward the back corner. The dog had located an old photograph that had somehow gotten wedged beneath the carpet. I picked it up and noticed it was an old photo of me.

"Wow, what was this doing in here?" I said aloud as I flipped the photo over and read what was written on the back.

"*Jayden Henner, New York City, 1988.*" I flipped the photo back over. I was standing in front of a building wearing a seventeenth-century costume, with a sword pointed at the camera as if I was about to engage in a fencing match. I was lunging forward with my right arm extended, and my left hand behind my back. I smiled as the memory of the moment returned to me. I was a cast member in a *Three Musketeers* play. At the time, I was twenty-two years old and a student at the American Academy of the Dramatic Arts. It was my last semester there. I had studied to become an actor. At the time, I believed I would go on to win a Tony or Oscar award. I smirked and looked closer at the photo, which revealed a woman standing behind me on the left side. She had on black, spandex biking shorts with an oversized MC Lyte T-shirt. I could make out the words *Lyte As A Rock* on her shirt.

"Wow, I wonder whatever happened to her?" I whispered to myself.

"You see this girl, Bo?" I showed the dog the photo he had found. He sniffed it again and wondered if it was a toy.

"She was something special, Bo, but I did her wrong. We had some really great times together back then. Bo, between me and you, this is the girl that I should have…" I paused. "I'll never forget her kisses. Her lips were soft and—"

"Who are you in here talking to?" Sylvia entered the room.

I was glad that I hadn't spoken too loudly. "Talking to Bo."

"You and that damned dog. I'm going to put both of you in the nut house. What's that in your hand?" Sylvia asked.

"Just an old photo that somehow got stuck under the carpet in the closet." I handed it to her, moved over to the window, and peeked out of it.

"Oh yeah; I've seen this before." Sylvia glanced at it before handing it back.

"I had plenty of big dreams back then."

"Yes, you were most certainly a dreamer. You believed that you would become some great actor."

"Hey, I'll have you know that some very well-known actors graduated from where I studied. I was serious about my craft."

"Name someone that you went to school with who is now a famous actor." Sylvia mocked me, and I became annoyed.

"I don't know. I have lost contact with everyone."

"I'll take that to mean none of them." Sylvia laughed, and it felt as if she had taken a few jabs at a part of my soul.

"Well, after I graduated I ended up the movie *School Daze*," I reminded her.

"Please. You were an extra, and you were only on the screen for a hot second, wearing dark sunglasses." Sylvia laughed again and antipathy toward her settled in my heart. I did not know why I felt so strongly about events of the past; I just did.

"Oh, hell no! Let me go get the tape and I'll show you that I was in the scene a little longer than one second." I wanted to prove her wrong.

"Please don't. It won't be necessary."

"I didn't think so." I squatted and rubbed Bo to cope with the thorns I felt I had been pricked with. "I did get a few walk on television roles as well."

"Yes, I know. You've shown me countless times."

"Well, it was a start. My agent worked hard to get me roles and I took whatever came my way," I said.

"You were a starving artist." Sylvia never embraced my dreams. She was realist and didn't entertain ideals she didn't believe in.

"You don't understand passion." I got defensive and wanted her to stop stomping on the grave of a dream that died when I met her.

"Don't go getting all tender about it. You should be glad that you decided to go get your MBA. At least you didn't starve to death."

A frown tugged at the corner of my lips. Then, for nostalgic reasons, I decided that I wanted to go through more old photos of my life before marriage, a son, and a mortgage. I exited the room and walked up the steps that led to the attic, with Bo trailing behind me. I flipped the light switch and grabbed a broom that was positioned against a wall. I had to knock down some silky spider webs before I could fully enter the space. I searched around until I found my trunk filled with photographs. I took the trunk downstairs into my office and closed the door. The first photo I pulled out was of me on stage with a group of my classmates. We were sitting on a sofa. I was sitting next to the same girl who was in the other photo I had found. My arm was around her this time. I was smiling, and she was too. It was after we had rehearsed a romantic scene. We both looked happy, and I remember that I had just told her that her kiss was tender and sweet. Throughout our kiss, I sensed that she might have had a deeper interest in me. I had suggested that we go out on a date, and she accepted my invitation. It was at the moment when she had agreed that someone asked us to pose for the photo. I remembered how one of the students had said that we made a cute couple.

I kept looking through old photos and realized that age and the summertime moisture that gets trapped in the attic had damaged some of the pictures.

"Thank God for the arrival of the digital age," I said to myself. I fired up my computer so that I could scan and preserve the pictures. As I sat at my desk going through the trunk, an unopened letter fell onto the floor. It was addressed to me, but I couldn't make out who it was from. I couldn't remember why I had kept it or never opened it. Curiosity got the better of me. I carefully pried the envelope open.

The note inside was dated 1988, and it was from the girl in the photo.

"Hey." Sylvia walked into the office and startled me.

"Hey, yourself." I pivoted in my chair.

"What's going on?"

"Nothing; just scanning old photos. By the way, I meant to ask who you were on the phone with earlier."

"I was gossiping with Ava."

"What's going on in her world?" I asked, only mildly interested.

"We were talking about something that happened when we were younger."

"I guess it must have been really funny, judging by the way you were laughing." I turned my back to her. I glanced at the letter and my pulse went into a sprint. I needed to hide it. I opened up a desk drawer and placed the envelope inside.

"It was," Sylvia said. She approached me, leaned forward, and hugged me. I kissed the back of her hand, which rested beneath my chin. Sylvia spun my chair around and straddled me. She looked deeply into my eyes and communicated her needs without uttering a sound. Although I was more interested in reading the letter, I knew it was wiser for me to go with the present moment and come back to it at some other time when Sylvia was not around.

"I'll be up to take a shower shortly," I said.

She kissed me, and walked out.

I sat for a minute before I removed the letter again. I exhaled, and searched my mind for an answer to my knee-jerk decision to hide it.

CHAPTER SEVEN

Bailey

Sitting on the terrace, I sipped wine and listened to sad love songs. The gentle bay breeze felt heavenly against my skin. My eyes focused on the perfect mixture of red, orange, and pink hues that seemed to hang above the glistening water. Right where the water met the sky, a hint of darkness developed as night began to creep in.

"This would be so romantic if I was wrapped up in a man's strong arms."

It was a glorious Thursday night; the weather was perfect; and I had the best seat possible. But still, I was lonely. One of my neighbors was entertaining, and the sounds of people laughing in the distance made me feel like a spy eavesdropping on their good time.

"I am too damn young and too damn pretty to be having a pity party all alone," I said aloud. I drained my glass and snatched my phone from the table.

Without thinking things through, I dialed Ava's number. I should've known I was wasting my time, but loneliness was a hard gulp to swallow.

"Ava, girl, what are you doing? Wanna go have a drink?"

"Girl, no!" she said.

"How come? It's such a pretty night out. What's the matter? Isaac won't let you out after dark?" I teased.

"Isaac ain't even here. He's out of town for a couple of days."

My ears instantly perked up. Her man was gone for a few days and she didn't think to call me? Sometimes I didn't know what to think about my good friend.

"So, aren't you lonely over there in that big ol' house all by yourself?" For a quick second, I felt a twinge of excitement, but it was short-lived.

"Bailey, puhleease! I'm so glad to have some peace. No, I ain't lonely."

"Humph. Well, I was thinking you might want to go out and enjoy this nice evening," I said.

"Bailey, we live in San Diego. Nearly every evening is nice. Now what's really going on?"

Sometimes, Ava's no-nonsense attitude was too much for me. She was always rushing you to the point. I really needed to get out more and meet new people. Although no one would ever accuse me of being shy, I stuck with Ava. I moved around better in familiar circles.

The truth was, women didn't really like me too much in the beginning. If they didn't take the time to get to know me, I rubbed them the wrong way. Ava understood me, and thank God, she wasn't threatened by me.

"Ava, I'm so tired of being by my damn self; that's what's really going on. Listen, I've accepted the fact that I won't meet a man sitting up in this house all alone. I don't like going out by myself. That wreaks of desperation, so I was hoping you'd want to go with me. We don't have to stay out too late."

"Baaaailey..." Her voice trailed off into silence, and I knew I had her.

"Ava, it's been so hard for me lately. I just really feel like some company. C'mon, you said it yourself, Isaac is gone. Let's go have a drink or some dessert," I begged.

"I don't feel like coming downtown."

The smile stretched across my face. "Okay; we can meet wherever you want."

"Shoot, Bailey, I was just about to get comfortable. I've got three chick flicks that I haven't been able to watch. Isaac never wants to see them. Hey, I have an idea, why don't you come over here and bring your PJs. We can eat junk food, binge on chick flicks, and—"

I cut her off.

"Ava, if my Mr. Right ain't coming to my place, do you really think he's gonna find me out there at your house?"

She laughed. "Okay, fine. Where are we going?"

"Don't sound so excited."

"Look, Bailey," she hissed. "I already told you, my evening was planned and it didn't involve getting dressed and putting on make-up," she added.

"But you are gonna put some on right? And Ava, wear something cute like that red wrap dress you have."

I hated when she threw any old thing on when we went out. I never wanted to say it, but I'd bet she didn't dress all drab when she went out with Sylvia. On second thought, they'd both been married like forever, so she probably did. Every single married woman I knew had allowed herself to fall off tremendously.

I remember back in the day, Ava used to work it. We'd hit the clubs, and both of us were turning heads. Even though in my opinion she'd married too young, she still had that mojo working. But as time passed, it seemed to me like she just let herself go, slowly but surely.

"If you're gonna be dictating what I can and cannot wear, I'm gonna stay right here in my comfy pajamas and you can go troll for men by yourself," Ava said sternly.

"Oh quit being so sensitive. Besides, we're not trolling for men. We're about to go out and absorb some of the great atmosphere in a trendy club or lounge."

"What a great sales pitch. I need to go get ready. Oh, and Bailey, no drama tonight, okay?"

"What?" I screamed. "I'm offended!"

"Well, maybe you should stay your offended butt at home."

"Fine, is thirty minutes enough time for you to get ready?"

"That should be fine."

A tingle fluttered through my body as I sprang from the chair. My mind raced with thoughts of what I should wear. Ava hated clubs, so I knew that was out of the question, but there were several lounges that I'd been wanting to check out.

Ava had a man, so she could keep it simple. But I was miserably single, so I needed to bring it every single time I walked out of my front door. I strolled into my walk-in closet, plucked out a blood red, fitted pencil skirt, and a shockingly bright, sheer cobalt top. It hugged my assets in all the right places, just the way I liked. Then I finished off my look with a sky high pair of tangerine stilettos.

I texted Ava the place where we'd meet and went to the kitchen to fill my flask. If I knew Ava, and I did, she'd be talking about her two drink limit, so, I needed to be able to sip some extra in the bathroom if necessary.

Regardless of how different Ava and I were, she was usually always down to try and help me out. I loved that about her, and although I wanted a man—no, make that a husband—desperately, I felt like she wanted the same thing for me.

I finished the drink and went into the bathroom to brush my teeth. Once I was dressed and adequately made up, I popped a breath mint in my mouth and headed out to meet Ava.

If I had known what was to come, I would've taken Ava's earlier advice and opted for the chick-flick marathon instead.

CHAPTER EIGHT

Ava

This was the type of shit that made me not want to fool with Bailey sometimes. She talked me into parking at her place so we could walk along the Gaslamp Quarter. I should've known better, but that seemed easier since neither of us knew exactly where we should go. I wished I'd never agreed to leaving my damn house in the first place. As I strolled along the busy street and back to her place, I wondered where this night had gone wrong.

I should've known by the way it started. We were outside her building and about to head over to what I called the tourist district. The area was San Diego's version of Bourbon Street in New Orleans, or Beale Street in Memphis.

"You gonna stroll in those?" I asked, looking down at her six-inch heels. She looked down too, as if she didn't realize what seemed out of place to me.

"Yeah, girl, you know how I carry mine. Besides, these are so incredibly comfortable."

I exhaled and rolled my eyes. I hated going out and being the hot girl's sidekick. I didn't wear what Bailey had told me to put on, but I really thought we were just gonna go somewhere and grab a quick drink. How cute do you need to look to sit at a damn bar? I should have known she was up to something more.

"I feel so underdressed."

Bailey eyed me up and down, her face twisting as she evaluated my outfit. "I told you what to wear, Ava. But you don't look bad."

"Wow, what a vote of confidence," I replied.

"It's not that big of a deal. I mean, look at me." She did a dramatic twirl that could rival that of any seasoned ballerina.

Of course, the minute she ended her pivot, a small crowd had formed. Men got on my nerves when they behaved as if they'd never seen a woman dressed in tight clothes. I wasn't hating on Bailey or anything like that, but seriously, it looked like she wore everything two sizes too small on purpose.

"Look, Ava, we've got company."

She smiled and giggled. When she batted her fake lashes and those gray contacts beamed, I thought for sure the guys would wise up and disburse. Instead, one of them stood next to me.

"Hey, who's your friend?"

I wanted to say, *She's standing right there. Ask her, not me! Especially, since you don't even know me!* Before I could answer his question, another guy slid close.

"You with her?" He motioned in her direction.

Bailey stood there grinning like a newly crowned beauty queen, basking in the glow of victory. I wanted to tell her we needed to move on, but she was busy talking to one of the lucky guys.

By the time the others realized they had acted too late, and I couldn't get them any closer to her, they went on about their business.

"Oh, this is my girl, Ava." Bailey finally looked over in my direction. "Ava, this is my new friend, Michael."

"Hi, Michael, nice to meet you."

I shook his hand, but he barely pulled his gaze away from Bailey. Instantly, I felt like a third wheel. I wanted to kick myself. She obviously didn't need me. We hadn't been on the street more than five minutes, and she had already picked up a stray.

It was a pleasant night. The weather was mild. Enticing aromas floated in the air from nearby restaurants, making my stomach growl. Dueling sounds of live music mixed with a DJ's beats, and laughter rang out into the night. I lagged three steps behind the new love birds.

To say I was irritated was an understatement.

"Let's head over to Croce's. It's right up there across the street to the right," Michael said. He pointed in the direction of several buildings farther ahead.

Bailey looked over her shoulder, and back at me. "Ava, Michael wants to go to Croce's; he says they have great live music there."

What's that got to do with me? I kept my thoughts to myself, and gave her a half shrug instead. Apparently that was enough encouragement for Bailey, since minutes later, we were headed up the street. Soon, we entered the packed restaurant.

As we squeezed by groups of people, all I could think was, *I should've stayed at home.*

Once we made our way to the front of the restaurant where the musicians did their thing, I was too through. By now, Bailey and Michael were hugged up and giggling like they'd known each other for more than an hour.

"Hey, Bailey, I think I'm about to call it a night."

"Huh?" She frowned, and leaned in closer to me.

"I *said*, I think I'm gonna call it a night!"

"You sure?"

She didn't even try to ask or convince me otherwise. I was so pissed. I could've stayed my behind at the house and watched my movies.

"You gonna be okay walking back to your car?" she asked.

"By myself?" I threw my hands to my hips and tilted my head.

Bailey gave me a pleading look with her cat-like eyes. I frowned to let her know I was not about to back down. She cowered a little, and eased closer to Michael. I watched as she whispered something in his ear. He looked over at me, then back at her, and nodded.

It was a damn shame to me that Bailey had to ask a stranger whether they could walk me back to her place so I could get in my car. I was so pissed at her.

On the stroll back to her building, I barely spoke to either one of them. When she said she desperately needed a man, I guess she meant it. I didn't care whether they went back to the restaurant or to hell, I was just glad when we made it back to the building.

"It was so nice meeting you," Michael said, like he just wanted me gone.

I was about to remind Bailey that I needed the sweater she had made me take off upstairs, but thought better of it.

"Okay, well, Bailey, you sure you're gonna be okay?" I asked her. I looked suspiciously in Michael's direction, who stood a few steps away.

Bailey smiled. "Oh, him?" She gave a dismissive wave. "We knew each other in high school." She looked back at him. "He's good people."

I've known Bailey for most of her life and I knew most of the people she knew. I gave her a look. *I was born at night, but baby, it wasn't last night.* With that, I pursed my lips, eased into my car, and backed out of the parking space.

I told myself to get ready for the sob story in the morning.

CHAPTER NINE

Jayden

I awoke before sunrise the following morning and prepared for my daily, five-mile run. I walked into my office and grabbed my cellular phone which I had been charging in there. I was about to head out of the door when I remembered the letter I had found in the attic. I turned around, opened my top desk drawer, picked it up, and walked out of the house. When I got into my car, I tossed the letter onto the passenger seat and drove a short distance to the track that I often jogged on. Once the car was parked, I opened the letter.

May 1, 1988

Dear Jayden

Where do I begin? I have so many thoughts and feelings that I want to share, but it is difficult for me to figure out what to talk about first. I guess the best place to start is with last night. The hip-hop party with MC Lyte and Slick Rick was fresh. I screamed so much that I lost my voice. Then, the soul food joint we hit after the concert was the bomb. The greens, short ribs, and cornbread were on fire. When it started raining as we were leaving, and we stood under the awning outside of the restaurant, you knew I had gotten cold. When you put your arms around me, I felt warm all over. I knew at that moment, snuggled up close to you, that you truly cared about me. As we ran to catch the bus, I couldn't believe the driver looked right at us and tried to keep going!

He was ill for that. I was so happy that you were able to make him stop. The driver was lucky that I didn't go to the max in front of everyone. I loved how you held me close to keep me warm from that blasting air conditioning. Again, a special feeling came over me. When we got back to the dorm, all sorts of crazy ideas were going through my mind. Especially after that kiss you gave me outside of my room. The kiss was hot, and the next thing I knew I was on fire. I guess you were too, because once I opened the door, you picked me up and carried me in. When we crash landed on my bed, I totally wanted to go all the way, but I wanted to be a good girl. I'm so glad that you understood that. I swear that I was not teasing you. I just want my first time to be when I am married.

Do you remember me telling you about my best friend, Sylvia? If not, she is the one who is attending community college and just broke up with her boyfriend. Anyway, I told her how amazing you are and showed her a photo of you. It was the one I took of you in Central Park back in October. She said that you were a gorgeous man and then looked at me and said, "Why does a dude who looks that good want to be with a geek like you?" Jayden, I swear I wanted smack her. She didn't stop with that comment either. Then she said, "A guy like him probably has girlfriends all over the city." I told her "Listen here, Freddy Krueger, Jayden is not like that!" I told her that you were legit and straight with me. I explained that you were a serious actor and that I believed in you. I shared so many wonderful things about you. She's my best friend, although sometimes she acts like she's jealous of me. Anyway, she wants to meet you, so I'll set something up soon.

Love Always, Cheryl

I placed the letter in the glove compartment for safekeeping. I recalled the day that Cheryl had given me the letter. It was a few days after she had put the brakes on going all the way. She thought I was mad with her and wanted to make things right. I was rushing to class when she gave it to me. I told her I would read it later, but I never got around to it. Eventually, I had her tell me what was in the letter. At the time, I was focused on trying to get a part in a new television show, *A Different World*, about black college life.

I exhaled, got out of the car, and went for my run. I thought about Cheryl the entire time. I wished that things between us had not turned out the way that they had.

When I returned home, Sylvia had gotten up and dressed for work. She was the director of human resources for San Diego Gas and Electric. I walked over to her and gave her an obligatory kiss on the cheek.

"How was your run?" she inquired. She stood in the doorway of the master bedroom and watched me get undressed as she ate her bagel.

"It was good. Nothing exciting," I answered before I headed into the bedroom for a shower. When I finished, I stepped out and found Sylvia holding out a towel for me. I dried off and oiled my skin.

"If I didn't have a meeting to be at this morning, I'd certainly stay and enjoy you all day long."

I looked deeply into her dark brown eyes.

"We haven't played hooky in a long time," I remarked and tried to recall the decade when we did such things.

"I know." Sylvia paused and abruptly switched subjects. "Would you like for me to cook you something to eat before I leave?"

"Yes, please."

"Do you want anything in particular?"

"A vegetable omelet would be nice."

Sylvia glanced at her watch. "Okay, I have enough time to make you one."

"I'll be there in a few minutes. It will not take me long to get dressed."

A short time later, I sat at the kitchen table and drank bottled water as I waited for Sylvia to finish my omelet.

"What do you want to do tonight?" she asked.

I shrugged my shoulders. "I don't know."

"Well, think of something for us to do." She flipped the egg in the skillet. "Now that Greg is out of the house, it feels different around here."

"Yes, we now have an empty nest." Hearing my words caused me to pause and fully process what that meant. Sylvia placed my food in front of me. I sliced the omelet with the edge of my fork.

"This might sound strange, but I feel like you and I need to reconnect. Lately, I've been feeling different."

"I don't understand what you're saying."

"Jayden, I feel like we haven't dated each other in a very long time. For the past several years, we've been operating like programmed robots."

"You do have a point; we have not dated each other since..." I stopped talking. An arbitrary thought entered my mind and forced me to focus on it. After reading that letter, thoughts of Cheryl had surfaced. As I thought about her, my pulse quickened as the memory of what it felt like to feel alive and desired sparked emotions that had been dormant for decades.

"Since what?" Sylvia interrupted my thoughts.

"Since a very long time." Then, from someplace deep inside, I heard a faint voice remind me that Sylvia and I had never truly dated each other.

"Jayden, it has not been that long, so you need to stop lying." I looked at Sylvia and analyzed what she'd just said. In her mind, she believed that we'd actually had a courtship.

"Perhaps. When was the last concert we went to? Can you re-member?"

"You know I don't like concerts. It gets too loud and I can't stand crowds." Sylvia finished her bagel, spooled off a paper towel, and dabbed the corners of her mouth.

"Think about it, and answer my question," I insisted.

Sylvia took a moment to think. "It was more than ten years ago; that much I do remember."

"Sylvia, we've never been to a concert." Feelings of regret sur-faced, but they were not triggered by the fact that I had not spent any significant quality time with Sylvia over the years. The regret was trigged by my own selfishness. I wondered why I had denied myself the experience of entertainment for so many years. *Why had I stopped living, and how did I get stuck in the valley of contentment?*

"Then that's why I don't remember."

"I think life got too busy for us. We had Greg, I was in graduate school, and my job had a lot of demands. Then, work got hectic for you and whenever we were together, Greg was the focus of our attention." I believed I had pinpointed how our marriage had survived without a real courtship.

"Hmm," Sylvia groaned, as if my words were a painful truth that she had come to accept on some subconscious level.

"Yeah," I whispered, but found the thought of enjoying an evening of entertainment with her to be dreadful. "I have a question for you."

"What?"

"Name something we've done together without our son that we both enjoyed?" Sylvia was about to quickly respond, but stopped. She had to think about the question. After an uncomfortable length of silence, I finally spoke.

"Hmm, I couldn't think of anything either," I admitted.

"Oh God, are we married and strangers at the same time?"

"That's really odd, isn't it?" I finished my meal. I looked at Sylvia and saw fatigue rising in her eyes.

"Well, that's something we're going to have to fix. There is plenty that we can do as a couple outside of dinner and a movie," she said.

"I'm sure there is. But perhaps we should find something that interests us individually as well."

"How did you change the subject to doing something we like individually when we were talking about doing something as a couple?"

I searched my mind for the answer to Sylvia's question. The answer I heard back was that I didn't truly want to spend time with her. I silenced that voice. It was a horrible thing to think. But the voice would not remain silent. It was going to be heard, whether I wanted to hear it or not.

"What are you thinking about? You have a distant look in your eyes." Sylvia's glare bore into me.

"You ever think about how we met, and why we got married?"

Sylvia recoiled has if I had pricked her with a thorn. It appeared as if my question had unearthed something that she had buried in the depths of her soul long ago. We both remained silent. The space between us suddenly felt uncomfortable.

CHAPTER TEN

Bailey

Michael Anderson was the truth! Two weeks after we put Ava into her car and sent her home, we were still going strong. I was so happy, I barely knew what to do with myself. I didn't want to jinx what we had, so I tried not to think too hard about it.

Quickly, my mind discounted all of the advice I'd picked up from the women's magazines. The most recent one said if you slept with a man within thirty days of meeting, you have a 90 percent chance of breaking up within a year. I was determined to prove that statistic wrong. After all, we had coasted right through the two-week mark. Two down, two and a half to go!

I never meant to sex these men the very first night we met, but usually the chemistry between us was so overwhelming, neither of us could help ourselves. And I always believe in taking chances.

As I sat in the conference room and waited for a meeting to start, I thought back to my first night with Michael. After we sent Ava off, we were already at my building, so going inside only made sense.

"You are so strikingly beautiful," he'd told me as we'd walked up to my front door. The energy between us was electrifying. He smelled really good, and I could tell quite a bit about a man from his scent. Michael told me he cared about his appearance more than most, and I liked that about him.

He planted a succulent kiss right on my neck, beneath my earlobe. That was my spot. How he could've possibly known that was beyond me, but I took it as a sign.

"But it's more than just your outer beauty; it's a sexiness that's so obvious," he whispered.

Many other men had told me that before, so I knew he was telling the truth. I had such a great feeling about him. He seemed to be in tune with things other men never noticed.

"The way you carry yourself, like a true lady, you just don't see that too much these days."

I had been thinking the exact same thing. I can't tell you how many times I'd seen women in pajamas and house shoes in Target. Michael was very perceptive, a sign of a good man.

He continued to shower me with compliments as I unlocked the door. It might have been him smooth talking me, but so much of what he said was so on point, I had to give him credit. It was like we were so in tune with each other.

"I just believe that a man deserves to have someone who makes him proud on his arm," I said as I unlocked my front door and pushed it open. "That's why I make sure to look my very best at all times."

Silence fell between us the moment Michael stepped inside my space. He looked as if he was awestruck. His eyes darted around the room—from the views, to my modern furniture, to the decor.

"Are those posters of you?" The posters were extra-large close-ups of my face. There was one in color, another in black and white, and a third done in three different shades. One hung over the mantel, another sat on an easel, and another hung on the stained brick wall that divided two massive windows.

I beamed with pride as he walked around the place. I had such a good feeling about him. Once he completed his inspection, he turned to me with a look of satisfaction across his face.

"I've been looking for a woman like you for a very long time."

There were no words to express how that had touched my heart. I told myself I'd do things differently this time. There might have been a meek smile on my face, but on the inside, an all-out parade was underway.

Later, it felt so right when Michael methodically peeled away my clothes and devoured my body as if I was a rare and exotic fruit.

The pyramid-shaped device in the middle of the conference table came to life with a buzz, forcing me to leave thoughts of Michael and me alone and refocus on work.

"Bailey Jones should be in the San Diego office," a voice said through the speaker.

"I'm here," I announced.

We were in the final stages of wrapping up a deal that would rent out the penthouse space in my building. The deal had been nearly a year in the making, and I was so glad to see it finally coming together.

Once it was finalized, it would mean a nice bonus for my staff and me. My paperwork was strategically arranged on the desk, and I had access to all of the tools I'd need. I was a beast when it came to work. I felt like I was born to work in corporate real estate.

Two hours into the grueling meeting, most of the conversation had been centered on additional perks my company would provide. I offered extra security, a private entry for executives, a gym with weekly massages, and mobile food services with a chef on-site three days a week.

The firm's realtor was going over numbers for the redesign to accommodate the gym when my personal cell phone chirped.

It was a text message from Michael. I smiled at the picture he had sent. It was a semi-nude of his body lounging on a bed and a text.

Wanted to give you a mental break in the middle of your workday. I miss you.

I was so touched by his gesture. Men didn't usually sext me. I had always been on the giving end.

Diane wheeled a small cart into the conference room. She knew to be as quiet as possible. We'd done this enough times for her to know the ropes inside and out.

As I listened to my counterpart spew out specs and numbers, I watched as Diane set up my lunch options. I pressed a button to mute the speaker.

"Thanks, Diane, I can take it from here."

"Let me know if you'll need anything else," she said, and exited the room as quietly as she'd entered.

After she left, I began to fix myself some of the chicken salad and other food she had arranged. As my conference call dragged on, thoughts of Michael stayed fresh on my mind. We'd been close to inseparable since the night we met.

By the time the conference call was over, I was exhausted. While I was sure we'd sign the necessary papers and get the client moved in, the last-minute haggling for whatever else they could get really took its toll.

I rose from my chair and walked back into the office.

"How'd it go?" Diane asked.

"We're almost there. I expect to close by next week."

That brought a smile to her face. She looked past me to the lunch cart and dishes I'd left. "Can I go and clean up in there?"

I turned to look back toward the room. "Yes. I think I'm done. Please make sure the paperwork is placed on my desk; we're not ready to file those away."

"Anything else? What about the leftover food?"

"Diane, you always do way too much. Please put it in the break room for the staff. I didn't touch half of it."

It was late afternoon, but felt much later. Being holed up in the conference room all morning for those meetings always gave me a bad case of cabin fever.

"I've got an offsite meeting; then I'm heading home early." I passed Diane wheeling the cart out of the conference room.

"Have a great rest of your day."

As I waited for the elevator, I dialed Michael's number. I was surprised when he answered.

"Oh, hey! I didn't expect you to pick up. I thought I'd leave you a sexy voicemail, thanking you for the picture you sent earlier," I said.

"Why wouldn't you get me?"

"What time is it?" I glanced at my watch. "It's nearly two in the afternoon. I figured you'd be busy."

"Oh, nah, I'm good. What's up with you? What are you doing?"

"I'm about to pass by a site and take it on home. My meeting this morning was grueling."

"I guess me keeping you up half the night didn't help either," he joked.

"Oh, that was well worth it. I'd gladly pay that penalty again and again."

It felt like the valet had my car waiting the moment I stepped off the elevator. I gave the driver a tip and eased behind the wheel.

"Babe, I'm in the car, so hold on a sec."

As the call switched over to my radio, I buckled up and prepared to do the drive by my next site. Michael told me how much he missed me and how fortunate he was to have me in his life.

Despite his kind words and his thoughtful text messages throughout the day, something about him still made me feel uneasy.

CHAPTER ELEVEN

Ava

"She doesn't want advice from me, I guess. I keep trying to tell her, you can't keep a man carrying on like that," I said.

Sylvia and I were at work talking about Bailey's man drama, and going over paperwork for the job fair our company was about to attend. I hated it when we agreed to go to job fairs, knowing good and well we had no openings.

"These single girls just don't know. They want a husband so badly that they don't stop to think about the first thing it takes to really make a marriage work," she said.

"Humph, ain't that the truth."

"But this Bailey girl, how does she ever expect to keep a man if she's so quick to jump in and outta beds?"

"Times are different now, so I guess she thinks that's how you keep them. I don't know. But you know I can't give her any sexual or relationship advice. As far as she's concerned, I've been sleeping with the same man for the past twenty years, so what do I know?"

"I guess that's a way to look at it, but she should also see that you've got what she wants. She's the one dying for a husband," Sylvia said.

She opened the glossy brochures so we could include them in the fancy packets containing information about our company.

"Well, maybe this new guy will work out. Dare I say, they're fast approaching an entire month together?"

Sylvia's thin eyebrows went crawling up her forehead. "You say that like it's some kind of impossible feat."

"Girl, for her, it is. See, you don't know Bailey like I do."

"I guess I don't. But you've known her for a real long time, right? How come we all never hang?" Sylvia asked. "Even when we go to happy hour on Fridays, she never comes along. What's up with that?"

I wanted to point out to Sylvia that she tended to be really hard on other women, and she was also the type who kept her circle small and close. There was no way those two would hit it off.

I shrugged her answer.

I kept aspects of my life separate. Bailey and Sylvia had met several times, but their personalities were too different. I felt the best way for me to be good friends to each of them was to keep the friendships apart. For years, it had been working just fine. They knew of each other, but didn't run in the same circles. This way, I was able to function in both of their lives.

"Most of Bailey's life is about trying to find a husband, so the things she likes to do wouldn't really interest you," I said. "Hell, they barely interest me."

Sylvia put a large stack of stapled packets between us. We'd been working in the main conference room all morning, and had something similar to an assembly line set up.

Earlier, when I suggested we get an administrative assistant to put the packets together, Sylvia wrinkled her nose. I realized she was right. We'd been locked behind quiet doors for hours, and that was just fine by me. It allowed us to get caught up on work and personal life drama.

"Honestly, I don't get how you can hang with so many single women," Sylvia said.

"What do you mean?"

"You have way more single friends than me. I feel like I have nothing in common with single women."

I tipped my head back and laughed.

"You sound like such an old, married woman," I joked.

Sylvia stopped what she was doing, tilted her head slightly, and frowned playfully. "You know what, you're right. I sure did, didn't I?"

We laughed together.

"Seriously, though, I've always believed that married women should hang with other married women. Think about it, when we have husband issues, what do we do?"

"We pick up the phone and call each other to vent," I said.

"Yeah, and can you not relate to everything I vent about when it comes to Jayden?"

I pursed my lips and gave her a knowing look. "You know good and well I can." Some of his antics crossed my mind, like his obsession with running marathons and the years he spent trying to drag her along.

"See, that's what I mean. Take your girl Bailey, for example. You can't sit on the phone with her and go on and on about how Isaac works your last, damn nerve when he's constantly misplacing his keys. You can't complain to her when Isaac leaves a trail of his clothes for you to pick up, and you damn sure can't complain to her when he's got his, rolled over, and left you hanging."

"Why not?"

"Because, for every single complaint you have about your husband, she's sitting up there thinking, 'Oh, that's not that big of a deal. I could handle that. If only I had a husband, I wouldn't give a damn what he did with his clothes, whether I got mine in bed last time, or why he keeps misplacing his keys. At least I'd have a husband!'"

I saw where she was going with that, and a part of me agreed with her. I could see how she felt like a single woman who was desperate for a husband might think of all the things she'd be willing to overlook, considering she was not in that position. It's easy to say what you would do when you're not dealing with the issue personally.

"And, I don't know much about your girl, but to me, when a woman is single, and badly wants a husband like that, eventually, she might not mind taking yours," Sylvia said, her eyebrows raised.

My eyes grew wide as I balked at that comment.

"Bailey is a little dense when it comes to relationships of the heart. But trust when I tell you, she does she not want Isaac. She wants a husband of her own. She's not the share-a-man type at all!"

"You never know, Ava. You just never know these days..." Sylvia warned. Her voice trailed off into silence that left us both in deep thought.

I didn't want to ask whether or not she was speaking from experience.

CHAPTER TWELVE

Jayden

I had just entered the home improvement store to pick up paint and supplies. I had decided to turn my son's bedroom into a cozy man cave. It was my do-it-yourself project, and I had set aside a $2,000 budget. I envisioned a new flat-screen television, a surround sound system, and a new theater-style recliner complete with a cup holder. I also had plans to place a poker table in there for occasions when friends visited.

I grabbed a cart and moved with purpose toward the paint section of the store. As I made my way, I heard someone call my name.

"Jayden." I looked over my left shoulder and saw Isaac, Ava's husband.

"What's up, man?" I smiled and gave him a brotherly handshake.

"A lot, but I'm dealing with the shit." He nervously shifted his weight from one foot to the other.

"That's all that we can do. Say, what are you doing on this side of town?" I pried.

"Handling personal business." Isaac was barely audible as he offered up his vague answer. By the secretive tone of voice he answered me in, I sensed that something was afoot, but I didn't know what.

"Are you okay, man? You sound as if the Secret Service is on a manhunt for you," I joked, then playfully punched his shoulder.

"I'm good. I just have a lot going on. What are you doing in here?" He pushed his hands deep into his pockets and began to rock back and forth.

"Well, now that Greg is gone, I'm converting his bedroom into my man cave. I want it to function as a place where I can escape from Sylvia and have fun with friends. We have to hook up again, man, and go to a San Diego Chargers game like we've always said that we would," I continued, changing the subject. I briefly thought about a time when I wanted to take Sylvia to a game, but I never asked. She wasn't into sports.

"If we can't get any good seats for the game, we should hit a sports bar. That way we'd be able to watch the game and buy a drink or two for some lucky ladies like we did last time. You remember; we had a blast." I laughed as I recalled the time we harmlessly flirted with two ladies at the bar.

"That was an interesting night. I'm certain we could have gotten into some serious trouble if we'd truly wanted to," Isaac admitted. "When those girls suggested that we go back to their place, I was like 'This is our lucky night.'" Isaac started to sound more like himself and a little less secretive.

"Yeah, man, that was a great and wild time. I had no idea that those girls were strippers."

"Man, we didn't get home until sunrise the next morning." Isaac slapped me on the back as he smiled at the memory.

"That's right," I said and snapped my fingers.

"I think it's a toss-up between that night and the time we hung out at the Hard Rock Café." Isaac looked around suspiciously as if to make sure he had not spoken too loudly.

"Now *that* was a night that will go down in the married men's history book," I agreed with him.

"Yeah, that was fun." Isaac's laugh began to fade.

"Yes it was."

"On a serious note, Sylvia didn't have a problem with you wanting to use Greg's bedroom for your personal use, did she?" Isaac redirected our conversation.

"What do you mean?"

"She didn't want to take the space for herself? She just let you have it?"

My ego gave an unapologetic answer. "First of all, I don't need her permission to let me do anything in a house where I pay the mortgage. That's called paying the cost to be the boss."

"All right, Jayden, I didn't mean to insinuate that you were not king of your castle." Isaac did not relish the notion of inadvertently insulting me.

"I can't have it any other way. How is Ava doing? And when do you guys plan on having kids? I'll probably be a grandfather by the time you two decide to have a child. You're not getting any younger you know," I harassed him.

"Ava is fine. As far as us having kids, it's complicated."

"What's complicated about it? Are you guys having trouble conceiving?" I asked and hoped that I wasn't meddling more than I should.

"Yeah, something like that." Isaac was once again being evasive.

"I'm sure everything will work out." I could tell the subject was an uncomfortable one. It always had been for as long as I'd known him. I had tried a number of times to get him to open up about the situation, but he wouldn't. Whatever the issue was, it was painful for him to openly talk about. At that moment, I heard someone call Isaac's name. When I looked in the direction of the voice, I saw a younger woman approaching. I had no idea who she was, and at first I thought there was another person named Isaac in the store. But when she met my friend's gaze and held on to it,

I knew she had found the person she had been searching for. When she turned down the aisle where Isaac and I were standing, I noticed that she was pregnant. She looped her arm around Isaac, rose up on her tiptoes, and kissed his cheek. She was an attractive woman in her mid-twenties, with mesmerizing hazel eyes and jet-black hair that angled sharply around her chin.

"Have you found the carpet for the nursery?" she asked him.

"Baby, umm, this here is an old friend of mine," Isaac introduced me without offering my name. He also gave me a paranoid glance and a slight nod which was a silent coded message that said I had to honor the loyalty of our friendship and follow his lead very closely.

"Hi, nice to meet you," I said, trying to conceal how stunned I was.

"I'm Denise," she said with smile that glowed.

"Well, it's nice to meet both of you, Denise," I motioned toward her tummy.

"Thank you." She rubbed her stomach affectionately.

"Baby, why don't you go and wait in the car for me? I'll be out with the carpet squares in a minute." Isaac reached into his pocket and handed Denise his car keys.

"Okay, babe. Nice meeting you." She pivoted and walked in the opposite direction. When she was out of hearing range, Isaac finally spoke.

"It's a long story, man," he explained and obviously did not want to go into the history of his relationship with Denise.

"Damn, Isaac. Does Ava know?" I leaned in and whispered the question.

"Hell, no. She has no clue and that's the way it needs to stay for right now."

"I don't know shit," I said, putting my hands up and backing off. I didn't want him to think that I would be disloyal and expose the fact that he had gotten his lover pregnant. "How far along is she?" I asked. Curiosity had gotten the better of me.

"Six months," he said. "Denise doesn't know that I'm married."

"What! Damn, man, you've gotten yourself into a real fucked-up situation."

"I told you that it was complicated," he reminded me.

"You're damned right it's complicated. How old is she?"

"Twenty-seven."

"You've got ten years on her. She got daddy issues or something?"

"No, that's not it. It started off as a friendship. We started talking, and I allowed myself to be vulnerable with her. I shared things about my life that I should not have. At first it was just innocent conversation, and then it turned into something else. I knew I should have used protection, but I got caught up in the moment." The blood drained from Isaac's face as he shared some of the details.

"I understand, but damn, you're caught in the crosshairs of a fucked situation."

"Look, man, just keep this under your hat for now until I can work this situation out, okay?"

"Dude, I got your back. I'm not going to say a word," I assured him.

"Good. I've got to pick up some carpet squares for the nursery. I'll be in touch."

"So does that mean we can't hook up for a San Diego Chargers game? I mean, with your resources being split like they are, you might not—"

Isaac interrupted me. "No, I'm okay in the money department. I'm down for going to see a game. Just let me know when."

"Cool," I said. I shook his hand before he departed and walked toward the flooring section with his head shamefully slumped between his shoulders.

CHAPTER THIRTEEN

Bailey

I t wasn't that I didn't need, or respect, Ava's advice. It was just that she had been married for so long, and I thought her guidance was kind of old-fashioned and outdated.

"I hear what you're saying, but this is different," I said and rolled my eyes once she looked down at her plate.

Michael and I were coasting into our one-month anniversary, and I felt like I had this. The last thing I needed was someone filling my head with issues about my relationship. Ava and I were enjoying lunch at Bay Park Fish Company. At least I was trying to enjoy it.

"You don't think it's too early?" she asked as she scrunched up her face and opened her mouth to bite the avocado she had just stabbed with her fork.

"That's what I'm trying to tell you. Back in the day when you two were courting, it may have been too soon. But honestly, Ava, I think Michael is going to be my husband. We are both mature and know exactly what we want. We don't need to wait; wait for what?" I shrugged.

I used the chopsticks to pick up the California roll and stuffed it into my mouth. I watched as Ava shook her head. Her mouth was full, but she seemed eager to respond to my comment.

"Girl, please! You act like I've been married for a million years!" Her eyes were ablaze with alarm. "I don't care how long I've been married. Men are still men, and I'm trying to tell you, something ain't right with how fast you two are moving. I mean, what's the rush?"

"Ava, if I'm happy and he's happy, how come you can't just be happy too? You know how long I've been waiting for someone like Michael to come into my life. Why ruin it for me?"

"Bailey, I'm not ruining anything. I'm simply telling you to think before you act. You've known this man for a hot minute and you're already talking about moving him into your place? Where's his place? What's up with his job? You'd be a good catch for any man. I don't see why you'd settle for someone who seems like he doesn't have his stuff together."

As Ava went on and on about Michael and his shortcomings, I couldn't help but feel like she didn't want to see me happy. The restaurant was packed and quite noisy. But I could hear Ava's hate loud and clear.

I swallowed back more than the food as she talked. Finally, I told myself to let her get it all out. I was not about to argue with Ava, but I needed her to understand that Michael was different.

"You don't know anything about him. And what kind of man just up and leaves everything to move into a woman's place? A woman he's only known for a few weeks," she added.

"Ava, my place is more than enough for us both. But I hear what you're saying, and I can kinda understand why you think we're moving too fast. I can assure you, though, he's good people. Remember, you only met him twice, and both times it was for a hot minute."

The expression on Ava's face told me nothing I could say would change her opinion about Michael. I ate the rest of my lunch and let her rattle off all of the reasons why I was making the biggest mistake of my life.

Usually when we finished eating, we'd sit around a bit longer, but today, I wanted to get out of there quickly. A waiter walked by, and I spoke up.

"Oooh, excuse me. Can you find our waitress? We need the check."

Ava drew her eyebrows together and watched the conversation between the new waiter and me unfold.

"What's up?" she asked, the minute he left our table.

"Oh, I need to get back so I can wrap up and get home."

"When does Michael get home from work?" she asked.

"Umm, he works from home." My eyes searched the busy restaurant in hopes of spotting our waitress.

"Wwhhhaaat?" Ava shrieked. "What kind of mess is that? What do you mean he works from home?"

I stopped my search and looked at Ava. I chuckled before I responded. I placed my palms on the table and inhaled deeply to calm myself.

"Ava, lots of people work successfully from home. My man happens to be one of them," I said.

Ava bit at her bottom lip. She studied me for a second, and then looked down at her watch again.

"Guess I'd better get back to the office."

I forced a smiled on my face. "Lunch was really good, huh?"

She nodded. "Umm hmm."

Later that evening, as I drove home, I couldn't let go of all of Ava's condescending comments about Michael and me. How did she know something was wrong when she didn't even know him? She'd met him twice for all of fifteen minutes.

When I walked into the house and a heavenly aroma swirled around and threw me into sensory overload, I wanted to literally drop to my knees, bow down, and give major props to the chef.

"Hey, baby," Michael called to me from the kitchen. "I didn't hear you come in."

He looked so comfortable and at home in my kitchen. He wore a wife beater T-shirt, a pair of plaid shorts, and one of my ruffled aprons. I loved having a man around the house. I didn't give a damn what Ava said.

The place looked different, but I was getting used to it. We had moved most of Michael's stuff in, so things were everywhere. But I still enjoyed coming home to him. I loved my man being there to greet me every day. What I loved even more was the idea that I had finally beaten the odds.

"Do you know what tomorrow is?" I asked later, as we sat on the couch cuddling and watching TV. I already felt so connected and close to him.

"Hmm, no. I can't say I do," Michael answered truthfully.

"It's our one-month anniversary."

I waited nervously for his reaction. It felt like forever and my heart was going faster than a NASCAR pro. When a low, sensual smile spread across his face, it nearly made me weak.

Later that night, as I lay in bed waiting for him to get out of the shower, I felt so at peace. I finally allowed myself to think about a future with Michael.

He walked out of the bathroom, smelling good and looking irresistible.

"Baby, the rest of my stuff should be here tomorrow," Michael said. He pulled back the crisp, white sheets on his side of the bed.

"Oh, okay, well, is there anything I can do?"

"Nah, you'll be at work. By the time you get here, it should all be good and I should be settled."

His cell phone rang and interrupted our conversation. He turned toward the phone and said, "Oh, I need to take this; it's my baby mama."

My head began to swim. I was totally taken aback. As he spoke into the phone, I scrutinized him. Michael told me he didn't have any kids. Suddenly, Ava's words flew around in my head like frantic birds trying to escape their cage.

He might as well have been speaking Arabic. None of his words registered or made sense. Honestly, I wasn't listening to his conversation at all. The voices in my head were screaming and drowning him out.

But the minute he hung up the phone, I turned to him. "I thought you said you didn't have any kids." I didn't even attempt to remove the salt from my tone.

CHAPTER FOURTEEN

Ava

"I'm telling you. I think the fool already lives with her!"

"What's up with her? I mean is she really that hard up for a man?" Sylvia asked. I could hear the sarcasm in her voice dripping through my phone.

"Girl, did I tell you she's got it bad or what? I dunno what the hell she thinks is gonna happen with some guy you pick up at a bar!"

"Wait, isn't that where she found what's-his-name?" Sylvia asked.

"Girl, that's where she finds 'em all. Then, when the mess don't work out, she's sitting up crying on my shoulder like a baby."

I couldn't think of any other way to get beyond my anger over Bailey's poor choices. Hell, her drama was enough to send me to a therapist! She didn't get it. How do you expect different results when you keep doing the same thing over and over again?

"How do you stand it?" Sylvia asked.

We had been on the phone discussing our favorite topic for nearly an hour. It had become such a sweet joke between us that Sylvia couldn't help but call for her weekly *As-Bailey's-World-Turns* update.

"Ava? Where you at?" Isaac yelled from the front door.

I used my hand to cover the mouthpiece on the phone.

"On the phone, you need something?" I yelled back.

"Nah, just letting you know I'm back is all."

"Who's that? Isaac?" Sylvia asked, "You need to go?"

"Nah, girl, his food is sitting in the microwave. I went on ahead and ate without him. I hate when he runs to Home Depot during the week. I mean, like what the hell are you gonna do? Build something in the back yard at night? It makes no damn sense." I huffed.

"Girl, what do they do that makes sense?"

We laughed.

"You've got a good point there. So, anyway, she's up there acting like she's ready to start picking out wedding dresses. And all I could think was you don't even know this man! He could be a serial killer for all she knows."

"Girl, this foolishness is too much for me. I'm glad she's your friend and not mine. I might be tempted to slap some sense into her," Sylvia said.

"Let's talk about something else. It just makes me sick to even think about her and the choices she continues to make."

"Ava, we've known each other for years; where do you know this girl from?"

I sighed. "Okay, well, long story short, our families were neighbors growing up. She's four years younger than me, and we've known each other since elementary school. Back then, we would hang out together, mostly because our mothers were friends. I remember they moved away when her mother ran off with some man. Then a few years later, they were back."

"You have got to be kidding me!" Sylvia screamed into the phone. She began to laugh. "Hold up, hold up a sec. Are you trying to tell me that this chick's mama ran off with another man? And the whole neighborhood knew about it?"

"Yes. That's exactly what I'm saying. Her father lived with his mother, or his mother lived with them. Either way, Bailey's grandmother lived in the same house. Well, one day, I came home from school just in time to see Bailey and her younger sister waving goodbye from the back of a station wagon's window. I asked my mom what happened and why were they moving. She said it was just Bailey's mom and the girls. The father and grandmother were staying."

"You know this is kind of tragic, right?"

"No, what's tragic is, two years later, we're sitting on the porch and a taxi pulls up. Bailey, her sister, and mother climb out and walk back into the house. Maybe a week later, an ambulance pulled up and her father was taken away. He had a heart attack and died. Then, her mother went away again, this time without the kids."

"Oh my!" Sylvia said. "How sad. No wonder the poor child has so many issues. Not only does she have daddy issues, but she's got trampy mama issues too." Sylvia laughed.

"Oooh!" I jumped when I realized Isaac was in the room with me.

"Y'all always on the phone gossiping! Don't you get tired of talking about your so-called friends?" he asked.

When his mouth twisted into a frown, it made me uncomfortable.

"Sylvia girl, I gotta go. Isaac just walked in."

"Hmm, okay; well, see you at work tomorrow," she said.

I hung up the phone and stretched my legs along the length of the bed. I hated when Isaac walked in on me using the phone. It didn't matter who I was talking to, he always accused me of gossiping.

"You coming to bed right now, or are you about to watch the game?" I asked.

My husband looked tired as he came and sat on the edge of the bed with his back to me. I wondered if work was wearing him down. "Want me to rub your shoulders?" I asked sweetly. I moved up behind him and touched his shoulders.

He flinched.

"Not in the mood tonight," he said dryly.

I wondered if he was acting funny since he'd overheard Sylvia and me talking about Bailey.

"Not in the mood for what? Hell, you haven't been in the mood for a good stretch of time now. What's going on?"

He yawned hard and long. He reached back and rubbed my thigh.

"Sorry, babe. I am working on a project at the job, and it's kicking my butt. I promise in a few months when this thing is all locked up, I'll take you away for a long weekend."

I felt better about that. My sweet husband had come back as quickly as he had vanished. I usually tried to restrict my calls when I knew Isaac was home. He didn't get how women communicated.

Unlike him and his friends, who probably never talked to each other on the phone unless they needed a question answered or the latest scores, that was how women bonded. We weren't talking about each other, but trying to get another perspective so we could be better friends to our friend in need.

Later that night, as I snuggled up close to my husband in bed, I had one last fleeting thought about Bailey and her poor choices.

I told myself I wouldn't spend my valuable energy worrying about her problematic life. I was grateful to God that my own was as close to perfect as I thought one could be. But the dark dream I had that night made me wonder whether it was Bailey's or my life headed for a tailspin.

CHAPTER FIFTEEN

Jayden

I couldn't sleep, so I got up in the middle of the night and went into my den. I shut the door and locked it. I stood on the chair and pushed back one of the ceiling tiles. I felt around until I found my secret stash of weed. It was a shameful and sporadic indulgence that I had developed in college. I grabbed my Bose noise cancelling headphones and iPod. I selected one of my favorite chill-out playlists and found a popular song by John Legend. I leaned back in my chair, lit my joint, and inhaled deeply. Video images of my life and marriage kept looping around in my mind endlessly. I wondered why I felt as if the only thing my life with Sylvia offered was a sense of wasted history.

Why didn't my marriage mirror my parents' relationship? They loved deeply, really liked one another, and took care of each other. That is how I hoped my marriage would be. But in reality, I dug deep within and faced the truth—the cancer that was infecting my spirit. The reason Sylvia and I got married was to avoid shame. At that time, we were in trouble and not in love.

I finished my joint and felt relaxed and at ease. It numbed me so that I didn't have to suffer the agony that my soul was in. I exhaled to ease the tightness in my chest. The next song on my playlist was "Don't Disturb This Groove" by an old-school group, The System.

"Damn," I whispered as I snapped my fingers and rode the wave of a distant memory the song brought forth. In my mind, I saw my-self with Cheryl. We were together when the song was out. She and I enjoyed doing the simplest things together. We'd talk, go for walks, and sometimes we would just spend time studying and being in the same space. Other times, we'd cuddle. She'd rest her back against my chest, and I would comb my fingers through her hair.

"What do you think we'll be like when we are in our forties?" she had asked once.

"I don't know. Hopefully we'll still be cool people." I massaged her scalp with the pads of my fingertips.

"I think we will. We won't be the type of people who forget how to have fun or lose sight of each other."

"I'm cool with that."

Cheryl turned over and looked into my eyes. "Can I ask you a very serious question?"

"You can ask me anything. You know that," I assured her.

"Are you disappointed about me wanting to wait until we are married before we make love?"

"I told you that I was cool with it."

"Sylvia told me I was crazy to make you wait." Cheryl rested her chin on the top of her hands.

"What did you say back to her?"

"I told her you were different, and weren't like that. I reminded her that I was a good church girl with morals. I told her I wanted my first time to be special and I was looking forward to a lifetime of special moments and wonderful memories with you."

"Well, you have broken a few of those so-called morals." I chuckled. Cheryl knew I was referring to the occasion when we had almost gone all the way.

"I'm being serious about this. I care about whom I give myself to. That should be important to you as well. I mean, would you really want a girl who has slept with a bunch of guys?"

"No, I wouldn't." I thought about the love I had for Cheryl and how we were alike in many ways. We came from similar, middle-class backgrounds. Our parents were educated and civil rights activists. We both worked our butts off to maintain our GPA and scholarship money. We liked the same music, and we both had a passion for the arts and humanities.

"Good. I want you to be my first, last, and only," Cheryl whispered sweetly and then kissed me.

"You like the idea of that, don't you?"

"What girl wouldn't? I think it's great that you're still a virgin."

"I'm probably the last virgin in my age group," I remarked, feeling a bit embarrassed.

"I'm sure you're not. If you've waited this long, a little more time isn't going to kill you. Besides, since neither one of us has actually had sex, it's not something we can honestly say we don't miss."

The song ended, and the distant memory faded. I was surprised that after all of this time, I still thought about Cheryl. Then, a crazy idea ran through my mind. I suddenly wondered where she was now. I had heard through a mutual friend years ago that she had moved out to California, but that was it. I sat upright in my chair, turned on my computer, and waited for it to boot up.

"Why haven't I thought to Google her name until now?" I spoke aloud to myself. Once the computer was up, I typed her name into the search engine. I saw her name pop up and clicked on the link. The next screen that appeared was for black women who were entertainment lawyers. There was a group photo of some women at a banquet of some sort. I studied the photo closely and immediately recognized Cheryl's smile.

"There you are," I whispered softly. She looked fantastic. I went back to Google, typed in her name again to see if she had a social media page. I found a link to a personal website. I clicked it and saw a better photo of her along with her bio. I learned that she was married, had two children, and worked for a movie production company in Los Angeles.

"Good for you," I said to myself. I was proud of her. There was an e-mail address where I could contact her, so I clicked it, but stopped myself. I recognized that I was feeling nostalgic and had to remember why Cheryl and I fell apart.

I leaned back in my seat and thought about the first time Cheryl introduced me to her friend, Sylvia. It was springtime, and she had come to the campus to visit her for the weekend. She stayed with Cheryl in her dorm room. I came over and met her. She seemed nice, and she wasn't bad looking. But Cheryl was, without a doubt, more attractive. We decided to grab a bite to eat at a local burger place. We got our food, sat down, laughed, and had a great time.

"So, Jayden, when do you think you and Cheryl will get married?" Sylvia asked.

"Sylvia." Cheryl elbowed her.

"What?" Sylvia shrugged her shoulders.

"It's okay, babe; the question is harmless," I said. "When we finish college."

"You mean you're going to wait until Cheryl finishes law school before you get married?" she asked.

"Law school?" I glanced at Cheryl, confused.

"I mentioned to her that my dad wants me to consider going to law school like he did. I'm not really thinking about that right now," Cheryl said.

"Hmm, so you really don't tell him everything." Sylvia landed a sucker punch to the core of my relationship with Cheryl. I laughed it off, even though in my mind I questioned why Cheryl had not mentioned law school to me. It caused the virus of betrayal to take root.

"I do tell him everything. I just had not gotten around to mentioning that to him." Cheryl attempted to clear up any misunderstanding.

"I understand," Sylvia said as she dipped a French fry into a little, white Dixie cup of ketchup.

"So, Sylvia, do you have a boyfriend?" I asked.

"Cheryl didn't tell you?" She looked at Cheryl and then at me.

"Tell me what?"

Cheryl rolled her eyes in annoyance.

"I am not into guys." Sylvia looked at me as she seductively swirled her tongue around a French fry.

"You're in to girls? Really?" I was excited.

"Jayden, I can't believe you just asked her that!" Cheryl kicked my shin.

"What?"

"Wow, you should have seen how big your eyes just got." Sylvia laughed. "I'm not in to women; that's nasty in my opinion. I like dating men with money who can buy me the finer things that I deserve," Sylvia explained as she dipped another French fry and sucked the ketchup off. She kept doing that the entire meal and I got aroused at the thought of her sucking on me that way. Cheryl didn't seem to notice or chose to ignore what Sylvia was doing, which was surprising.

A few days later, when Cheryl and I were spending quiet time together, we started making out. As I kissed Cheryl, I thought about Sylvia's lips sucking on me. I asked Cheryl to go down on me.

She immediately stopped kissing me. "I don't do that."

When she denied me, I felt resentment stir in my heart. I still loved her, but had to fight to keep my bruised ego in check so that my disappointment would not mature into a grievance.

CHAPTER SIXTEEN

Bailey

"So, what's going on with your job again?" I moved all the way into the living room where Michael was watching a game. If he detected the attitude in my voice, he never said anything about it. The place smelled awful, and I was more than slightly irritated.

"Aww, shoot, I'ont know." He moved his arm in a sweeping motion as if to dismiss my question. Michael craned his neck to look around my body. I stood and blocked the large screen TV, on purpose.

"C'mon, babe, you makin' me miss the game," he grumbled and frowned. He used a massive paw to grab a fist full of popcorn, stuffing it into his mouth. That's when I took in the disturbing sight before me.

I looked around at the empty beer cans; a couple of them were strewn across the floor. From what I could see, his entire day had been spent in that very spot. There was the box of Cocoa Puffs cereal on the floor next to the coffee table, and the large mixing bowl with a small pool of leftover chocolate milk was still sitting there too. In addition to that, an empty carton of pizza rolls was sticking out from beneath one of the cushions on the sofa. And if that wasn't enough, a half-eaten sandwich sat abandoned on a plate next to a half-empty glass of iced tea. Several chips had fallen off the plate.

My place looked downright nasty. Michael didn't seem the least bit fazed. He had returned his attention to the game. Ignored as if I hadn't said a word, I sulked out of the room and wondered what I had gotten myself into. As I retreated to the bedroom, I thought back to the other night, and his lame response to the question I had asked about whether he had any kids.

"Nah, girl! I told you I'm not with her."

I'd stared at him like he must've thought I was stupid.

"Michael, that's not what I asked," I'd snarled. "I didn't ask you whether you were with anyone. Shit, you live here with me! That's obvious, isn't it?"

"Aww, girl! I know you ain't tryin' to act all mad and shit. You know I ain't tryin' to be with nobody but your fine ass."

I couldn't believe he was joking at a time like this.

"I clearly asked if you had any kids and you said no. Now I gotta listen to you talk to your baby mama on the phone, in my bed? In our bed?"

"Oh, girl, that's Keisha. She real cool and down-to-earth. Now if it was Dawn, I could see you being all bent outta shape. That trick is ghetto as hell. I'ont know what I ever even saw in her ass. But you know what they say; you can't trust a big butt and a smile." He had the nerve to laugh at his own lame joke.

All that flashed through my mind was, *This man has more than one kid and more than one baby mama?*

My eyes narrowed to slits; anger flashed through my heart like an electric jolt. I shook as I'd jerked my body away from him, turned, and pulled the covers up to my chin.

Back in the present, as I sat alone in my room and heard Michael's screams as he watched the game in the living room, I wondered what else he had kept from me. I didn't want to start second-guessing my relationship. It had been so long since I'd had a man, I felt like maybe I should try to look the other way.

But the truth was, it wasn't the fact that he had kids, it was the fact that he had obviously lied about it. I sighed hard, pushed the thoughts from my head, and got up to change my clothes.

I riffled through the dresser drawers until I dug out the lounge-wear I wanted. I found my iPod and plugged it up to the boom box on the nightstand next to my bed. As sounds of Jill Scott's "Crown Royal" floated through the air, I went to take a shower.

"Is it so bad if he has kids?" I said aloud. "These days, it's gonna be near impossible to find a man who doesn't."

After the water's steam clouded the bathroom, I undressed and climbed into the shower. I was exhausted. After a long and tough day at work, I didn't need to come home and find my unemployed boyfriend lounging and vegging out on sports and junk food.

I didn't know when tears began to mix with the hot water, but I allowed them to flow. I cried for everything—all of my frustrations, all of my pain, and my fears of being alone. I couldn't give up on Michael. I knew that would only prove Ava was correct.

Using my palms, I wiped away my tears and told myself I needed to be strong. Okay, so maybe Michael wasn't perfect, and was far from Mr. Right. Maybe he wasn't the man he made himself out to be in the beginning. The bottom line was, we had been together for more than a month, and I needed to make sure I did everything possible to keep us going strong.

One minute I was convincing myself he was worth the fight, and the next, I turned to see his chocolate abs with water drizzling down his fleshed ridges.

"I could tell you needed some extra attention," he said.

Before I could respond or even react, his mouth covered mine.

He kissed me like he was starving. I kissed him back. I kept my eyes closed and completely gave in. When he took me into his arms and lifted me off my feet, I suddenly didn't care how many children he had fathered.

Michael clutched my thighs as he backed me into the shower tiles. Our kissing had become more intense. He went from my lips to my neck, and then down to my chest.

I kept my legs wrapped around his waist, and my arms around his neck. As my back stuck to the tiles, he used his tongue to work me over and made me not give a damn what was wrong with him.

"Oh, Michael baby; oh, baby," I cried.

As music played in the background and hot pellets of water danced against our skin, my man made love to me like no other man before him.

Ripples of pleasure ran up my legs and through the rest of my entire body. He never stopped. I shivered and trembled as he thrust himself in and out of me. I was so happy to have him, so happy he had chosen me. In that moment, all of my insecurities and fear over our relationship mixed with the water, and washed down the shower's drain.

CHAPTER SEVENTEEN

Ava

I stared at the man whose lips trembled as he sat twisting his hat in his hands. My job was to sit quietly and observe as a backup and witness in case the incident was ever questioned.

"As you see here, Mr. DeLeon, we have photos of you on jet skis; here is another where you are barefoot, but balancing several bags in your hands. Then, there are these where you are on an ATV. Oh, and there's this one that clearly shows you climbing up to the roof to adjust your satellite dish." Sylvia spread the photos out on the desk for the employee to see.

"I can explain all of those," he replied.

Sylvia shook her head. "Oh, I don't think you understand. We've long passed the point of explanation. Our records indicate that you and your doctors claimed you were disabled. The company can take legal action based on these photos alone."

"But, my family—"

"Yeah, is that the same family you were out on the lake with when you were supposed to be at home and incapacitated?"

I wanted Sylvia to wrap this up. I hated when we had to terminate people, but Sylvia seemed to be able to find some special joy in it with no problem.

"So what do I have to do to make this all go away?" the man asked.

Sylvia sat back in her chair. She exhaled and stared off as if he had several options and she needed to consider the best one.

"Well, you can quit."

The horror in his eyes scared me. I wondered what he expected her to say. When he began to shake his head, I knew this was going to be a very long session. Then, the conversation took a sudden turn.

"I think I wanna talk to my lawyer," Mr. DeLeon said. He sniffled a few times and his back suddenly straightened.

I just wanted the session to end. If he had quit, we would've been able to avoid a long, drawn-out process. But when he started talking about a lawyer, that meant it was out of our hands.

At his announcement, Sylvia closed the folder she had in front of her, and rose from her chair. I followed her lead and did the same. She used her hands to smooth out her dress.

"Then we look forward to seeing you in court, Mr. DeLeon."

I watched as the man pulled himself up from his chair, and then walked out of the conference room. The moment he closed the door, Sylvia turned to me. "Men are so damn simple!"

I felt like I was finally able to release the trapped breath I'd been holding tightly.

"That fool really thinks he has a chance? He was caught red-handed defrauding this company. I will turn his case over to the right department and he's gonna wish he would've taken me up on my offer."

"Dang, Sylvia, you are no joke, huh?"

"You can't be. If people smell fear, girl, they will walk all over you and take any damn thing they want." She moved closer. "It's like Jayden's simple behind. I've had the private investigator look into him a couple of times for me."

I was stunned. I couldn't imagine hiring a private investigator to do such a thing. I threw a hand onto my hip. "You did what?"

"Yeah, girl, I don't play that mess. He's lucky that when the guy followed him, all he did was go to a few titty bars and the casino," Sylvia said. "It's not like it cost me anything. I helped the company's private investigator get the job, so every once in a while, he'll do me a solid."

I started cracking up. "I can't believe you had someone follow your husband around!"

"Girl, please! I know everything there is to know about his behind. Just the other day, I walked into his study behind the cleaning lady. I turned on the computer, checked the history cache on his monitor, and saw that he had looked up his ex-girlfriend. I made a mental note to get Brandon Rouse on the case!"

Sylvia had started to gather the folders and papers from Mr. DeLeon's session. She didn't miss a beat as she explained to me how she'd been spying on her husband.

"Yeah, so from what I could tell, he looked her up. I don't know whether he contacted her, but you'd better believe I'm waiting on the intel from that. Let me find out he's been trying to reclaim his glory days," she said.

"So you think he's doing something?"

"Humph, he ain't got the balls to do nothing. I know that. Don't get me wrong, I don't go looking for trouble. Like I said, when I had the detective follow him, I was glad to learn my man wasn't running around on me. But what I'm trying to tell you is this, Ava." She stopped what she was doing and looked me in the eyes. "When you've been married for as long as we have, you can't sit back and assume he's doing the right thing all the time. Now I'm not saying Jayden ain't never stepped out on me. I'm just saying that three years ago, and as recently as six months ago when the investigator looked, he wasn't doing a damn thing."

"So, why do you think he was looking up his ex then?"

"'Cause he's a man who's battling middle age. Think about it. We're empty-nesters now, so he's probably a little restless and bored. Like I said, let me find out he's been communicating with Cheryl and heads are gonna damn sure roll."

As Sylvia and I left the conference room, I couldn't begin to wrap my mind around what she had done. I feel like if you have to have your man investigated, then maybe you and that man don't need to be together. For the first time, I started to think about the friends I had. Sylvia and I had always made fun of Bailey, but shit, I didn't know who was worse.

Who gets a private investigator to spy on her husband, especially if he hasn't even given her a reason to be suspicious?

"I've always been that way. Ain't no man gonna get the best of me. Hell, forget a man. Nobody," Sylvia boasted as we waited for the elevator, like she could read my mind. "You want me to see what Isaac's been doing?" she offered.

"Nah, I'm good. Besides, I don't handle surprises well."

CHAPTER EIGHTEEN

Jayden

Late in the evening, I sat in bed with the remote in my hand and watched a rebroadcast of the movie *Bad Boys*. Sylvia was in the bathroom taking a shower. When she finished, she entered the bedroom wearing her robe. She crawled into bed and snuggled up next to me. She began placing sweet kisses on my shoulder and neck.

"Turn that off," she whispered and rubbed my thigh.

"Umm hmm," I said and ignored her request. To make sure that she had my full attention, Sylvia straddled me and began kissing my neck. She moved down to my chest and then my abdomen. When she arrived at my silk boxer shorts, my cell phone buzzed. I glanced at it and saw that the caller ID read *Jail*.

"Who is that calling you this late at night?" Sylvia asked while tugging at my boxers.

"Looks like a wrong number," I said. Once my boxers were off, I repositioned myself so that I was more comfortable. Sylvia began kissing my thigh. Before Sylvia could get started, my cell phone rang again. I reached over, picked it up, and again saw that the call was coming from a correctional facility. I ignored it and set it back down.

"Don't you want to fool around?" Sylvia now had the full weight of her body resting on me and purposely spoke in my ear. As I listened to her tender words, the phone rang a third time.

"Why in the hell is your phone ringing like that?" Sylvia recoiled from me as if I had poked her with a branding iron.

"I don't know." Then I thought that something had perhaps happened to our son, so I answered it before it stopped ringing.

"Hello?"

"Hey, can you talk?" Isaac whispered.

"Isaac? Hold on a second for me, man." I sensed something was very wrong by his tone of voice. I briefly glanced at Sylvia and shrugged my shoulders. I had no idea why Isaac was calling. I got up and headed in the direction of the master bathroom for privacy. Sylvia angrily trailed me and snatched my phone out of my hand.

"Who the hell is this?" Sylvia shouted into the phone.

"What the fuck is wrong with you?" I reached for my phone, but she turned so that I couldn't grab it from her.

"Oh, hey, Isaac," she spoke bitterly. "I hope you know that you're intruding on our privacy."

"Give me the phone." I finally snatched it back. "What the hell has gotten into you?"

"If that had been my cell phone ringing at this time of the night, wouldn't you get at least a little suspicious?" Sylvia lowered her eyes to slits.

"You should know me better than that," I said as I walked into the bathroom and shut the door.

"Yo, you still there, man?" I asked.

"I apologize for calling you like this, Jayden, but I really need your help." Isaac sounded distressed.

"What's going on?"

"I'm in jail," he said.

"What the fuck are you doing in jail?" I asked before taking a seat on the edge of the bathtub.

"It's a long story. I'm in need of bail money. I promise you I'll get it back to you first thing tomorrow morning."

"Where are you at?" I asked.

"I'm down at the Central Jail on Front Street," Isaac explained.

"How much is your bail?"

"Eight hundred," Isaac said.

"I got you. Give me about forty-five minutes," I said.

"Yo, don't tell Sylvia where I'm at."

"Dude, we're frat brothers; you don't have to tell me that," I reminded him. "But you know that Sylvia is going to call Ava."

"I'll deal with that part later."

"Let me get dressed. I'll see you in a bit," I said and hung up the phone. I inhaled deeply and exhaled. I sat for a moment, lost in thought, before I got up and walked out of the bathroom.

"Turn off your phone and come back to bed," Sylvia insisted and rubbed a spot next to her.

"That has to wait," I said and moved toward my closet.

"What? I know you don't have an attitude because I grabbed the phone from you." Sylvia's voice raised several octaves.

"No, I do not have an attitude, even though the phone thing was a bit over the top."

"Okay, maybe I overreacted a little, but can you blame me?" Her tone switched to one that was more gentle and sweet.

"It's not you that I'm against, Sylvia; it was your behavior that I didn't like," I said.

"Where are you going?" She rushed out of bed and followed me into the closet. I grabbed a pair of jeans and a polo shirt.

"Isaac's at a bar and has had one too many drinks. The bartender took his keys and told him to call someone to drive him home." I made up a lie that I hoped she would accept.

"Why is he out drinking by himself? And why doesn't he just call Ava?" Sylvia asked.

"He mentioned something about losing a big account and I don't know why he did not call Ava," I lied again.

"Ava is probably sick of his bullshit." Sylvia accepted the lie I told and walked back into the bedroom. I put on my clothes, grabbed my keys, and headed for the door.

"Wake me up when you get back so we can finish what we started," Sylvia said as she got underneath the covers and picked up the television remote.

I left the house and drove as quickly as I could to an ATM. I withdrew the money I needed and then headed toward the jail. When I arrived, I walked up to the desk sergeant, explained who I was and why I was there. I went through the process of paying Isaac's bail and then sat and waited for an hour for them to release him. When he finally came out of lock up, he walked over to me and gave me a brotherly hug.

"I never want to see another jail cell for as long as I live," Isaac said as we stepped outside.

"I don't think anyone who is locked up wants to be there."

"You've got a point there. Look, I need a ride back to my car." Isaac massaged his temples with the pads of his fingertips.

"Where is your car?" I asked.

"In front of Denise's house."

"All right, I'll give you ride over there. But you know I've got to ask. What the fuck happened?"

"I'll tell you when we get in the car."

Isaac told me which direction I needed to drive in. Once we were on our way, he began to talk.

"So, I go to see Denise, to check on her, right?" Isaac said.

"Okay," I said and waited for the story to unfold.

"I arrived, put my key in the lock, and discovered that it didn't work. So I was like what the hell is going on? I kept trying the key, thinking that maybe the lock was jammed or something. When I couldn't get it opened, I called Denise but she wouldn't answer. Next thing I knew, the police rolled up. They got out of the car and rushed towards me like I was a suspect who had just robbed a liquor store. They told me to get on the ground with my face down. And I was like, what the fuck for?"

"What the fuck was wrong with the police?" I asked as Isaac told me to make a right turn.

"I'm trying to tell you." Isaac paused. "The situation was surreal. The police screamed at me to get down, but I was half-cocked and started asking questions. When I didn't do as I was told, they pulled out their service revolvers. When I saw that, I knew they were not playing around, so I got down on my knees with my hands held up. Those bastards pushed me to the ground, put their knees in my back, and handcuffed me."

"Damn." I shook my head in disbelief.

"They stood me up and searched through my pockets. I kept asking them what in the hell was going on. Then Denise finally opened the front door and said, 'That's him, officers.'"

"She set you up?"

"Man, that bitch put a restraining order against me. She showed the police officers the document, and once they verified my identity, off to jail I went."

"What is that all about?" I asked.

"I don't even know. When I started shouting questions at her, one of the officers walked her back inside the apartment while the other one walked me to the squad car."

"Damn. What are you going to do?"

"Find out what the fuck is going on," Isaac said.

"Man, you sure you want to keep fooling around with Denise?" I asked, concerned for his welfare.

"How can I not? She's pregnant with my child."

"Your ego may not want to hear this, but are you sure it's yours?" My question lingered in the air like a foul smell that wouldn't fade.

"I hadn't considered that," Isaac finally said. "My car is right up here."

I pulled up to the back of his car and stopped.

"What did you tell Sylvia when you left the house?"

"I made up a story about you being at a bar having too much drink because of some big account you lost."

"That's good. I owe you one." Isaac opened the door.

"You good?" I asked.

"Jayden, would it be too much to ask for you to hit a bar with me? Now that you mentioned where I was supposed to be, I could really use a cold one."

"Yeah, we can do that."

CHAPTER NINETEEN

Bailey

Two weeks had passed since the last time I tried to talk to Michael about his job and I was still no closer to an answer. There was no doubt in my mind that he was unemployed, but he would change the subject every time I brought it up.

What I couldn't figure out was how he always seemed to have money. As I sat at my desk, I tried to tell myself that as long as he wasn't doing anything illegal, I shouldn't worry about it.

I had enough on my hands with the new penthouse tenants in the building. My mind should've been focused on the new list of items they had requested in renovations, but I couldn't stop thinking about Michael.

When I looked up at Diane's stone-faced stare, alarms went off in my head.

How long had she been standing there? Was she waiting on my approval for something?

Had she asked a question? My mind was really blank.

"I'm sorry," I began, with a half shrug.

"The Spanish tiles," she said sternly. "Did you or did you not approve them?"

Diane's body language told me she didn't have time for whatever had me so preoccupied. She was used to me being on my toes at all times. There was very little room for slackers in our fast-paced office. And usually, I was on my game. But today, thoughts of my relationship, and where it was headed, had slowed me considerably.

"Oh, yes. The Spanish tiles. I did. I know that's a line item that could've come from our warehouse, but, yes, I did approve them."

Diane didn't ask whether something was wrong with me. Her eyes fell to the list she held in her hands and she rattled off several additional questions.

When I couldn't take it anymore, I rose from my chair. "Listen, I'm not feeling well. We're gonna have to finish this up tomorrow," I said.

She didn't respond, so I looked up and saw the expression on her face.

Diane's eyebrows bunched together. "Tomorrow is Saturday." All that was missing was the dramatic eye roll.

"Well, Monday then." I gathered my belongings, straightened my desk, and snatched my purse from the bottom drawer.

"Leaving for a late lunch?"

"No, I'm gone for the day. Enjoy your weekend, Diane," I said over my shoulder. I sauntered passed her and out of the door.

It didn't matter to me whether she wanted to stay and work. There were burning issues I needed to address with Michael. As I walked to the elevator, I told myself all of the reasons why I needed to pin him down on one topic or another. What had happened to his job? What was he doing for money? How had my house become his bunker? And why every time I tried to talk to him, did we wind up in bed?

Thoughts of Ava and her warning came to mind, but I pushed those aside. I already had enough on my plate. Minutes later, as I eased behind the wheel, I considered calling Michael. There was a part of me that wanted to give him the chance to explain every-thing away, but in the end, I decided it was best to surprise him.

Catching him off-guard would help ensure that he wasn't lying. In my heart of hearts, I didn't believe he was doing anything wrong, but a bunch of little things put together was just as bad as any one, massive, glaring issue.

The forty-five-minute wait in traffic gave me ample time to cool off. Was it so bad that he didn't have a conventional job? It wasn't like he was hitting me up for money. What difference did it make that he stayed at home? I had used similar words to defend him to Ava. Why was I suddenly tripping on the man? The little voice in my head told me that I was looking for a reason to sabotage my relationship and that was no way to find a husband.

Instead of turning onto the street that would take me home, I kept driving and pulled into the grocery store parking lot.

"I'll fix us a nice romantic dinner, and while we're eating, I can tell him about my concerns. That way he's not threatened by my need to get more details."

My idea seemed perfect. It made absolute sense. I'd get some lobster tails, potatoes, and a great bottle of wine. Maybe two bot-tles, and a chocolate cake for dessert.

As I walked around the grocery store, I began to fall more in love with my idea. Unfortunately for me, the lines were atrocious. I flicked my wrist to look at my watch. *By the time I get out of here, it'll be as if I'd stayed for the rest of the work day*, I thought.

Since there was nothing I could do, I waited my turn in line and imagined how surprised Michael would be over dinner. Lately, I'd become a woman I wouldn't want if I was a man.

Most days I'd walk through the door with a sour expression on my face. Once inside, I'd quickly scrutinize what he'd eaten and the mess he'd made. Then, when Michael didn't answer my questions to my satisfaction, I'd storm off to my room and question the stability, or lack thereof, of our relationship.

As I inched forward in the slow-moving line, I vowed to do better. The goal was to earn Michael's last name, not turn him off as a result of my attitude.

By the time I'd paid for the groceries and gotten back in the car, I felt better about my new perspective. What surprised me most was the fact that I had arrived at a plausible solution without getting Ava to weigh in.

I smiled at my reflection in the rearview mirror as I backed out of the space and made my way home. I had a good man, and soon, we'd be married.

Once I parked in the garage, I surveyed the bags and thought about whether I could carry them in myself. The idea was to catch Michael completely off-guard and give him the biggest surprise of the week.

After several minor adjustments, I left my computer bag in the car and grabbed the shopping bags and my purse. My heart began to race a little as I stood in the elevator and watched the numbers climb higher.

We needed this romantic kickoff to the weekend. And since I already knew how disagreeable I'd been all week long, I just knew Michael would welcome the surprise for a change.

I unlocked the door, picked up the bags, and walked into the house. Suddenly, I realized Michael had been working on a surprise of his own.

It wasn't until I heard the wine bottle burst when it hit the floor, and I felt droplets of liquid splash my legs that it sank in. This wasn't a dream; what I saw was actually real.

CHAPTER TWENTY

Ava

I was determined not to call or contact Bailey. It wasn't that I was giving up on my childhood friend. Lord knows, I wouldn't do that. But I was trying to remove myself from the drama that was her life.

She begged for advice, but never listened when I gave it. As a matter-of-fact, sometimes she made me wonder why she even asked for the advice, if she was gonna continue to do the opposite of what I suggested. In addition, she continued to make the same simple mistakes over and over again, failing to learn from any of the experiences. I was completely disgusted and tired.

Weeks after Sylvia had confided in me that she spied on her husband, one thought rolled around in my head. Day and night, all I could think about was the power of knowing what someone was doing without being in their presence. Although I didn't want to get too wrapped up in Bailey's relationship with Michael, I had been thinking about taking Sylvia up on her offer.

No, I did not want her to spy on Isaac, but maybe what I could do was have her set her private detective guy on Michael, as a favor for Bailey.

For days, I'd been trying to think of a way to present the idea to Bailey. I knew it would take some work to sell it to Sylvia too, but Bailey would probably take more offense at the suggestion.

"What's for dinner tonight?"

Isaac's voice caught me off-guard. I didn't realize he had come home. I turned to face him and hoped he'd remember that I didn't cook on the weekends.

"You've been acting kinda strange lately; what's going on?" I asked my husband.

His eyes seemed shifty. He never really made contact with mine before he rushed over to the refrigerator. I watched as he pulled it open, stood back, and peered inside. He rubbed his stomach with his free hand and yawned.

"Need something to eat," he said.

"Well, what do you want?"

I sat at the table as my husband moved around the kitchen. He closed the refrigerator door, and then walked to the pantry. A few seconds later, he left the pantry, and moved toward the stove. He opened a cabinet door, but I figured he didn't find whatever he was looking for, since he came out empty-handed.

Finally, he came over and sat next to me. When Isaac sighed hard and heavy, I started to wonder what could be weighing him down. We weren't wealthy, but we were more than comfortable. We'd both been on our jobs for a number of years and enjoyed freedoms that most workers only dreamed about. Our house was nearly mortgage free, and we bought brand new cars every two years. We didn't have to dodge bill collectors and we didn't have to worry about whether we had enough money in the bank.

"You want me to fix you a drink?" I asked.

His eyes shifted over to me and he stared. He looked at me for so long, I became uncomfortable under his gaze. When he replied with a shrug of his shoulders, I wasn't sure whether I should move.

My body stiffened when I noticed his eyes twitching. I reached out and took his hand into mine.

"Isaac, baby, is everything okay? What's going on with you?" I asked softly.

His Adam's apple bobbed as he swallowed a couple of times, but still there was no answer. I tilted my head forward slightly and gave him a cheeky smile. "You know, I think we may need to take a vacation. Maybe we can go back to Jamaica. Remember how much fun we had at that Sandals Resort?"

That suggestion brought a smile to his face. At the sight of it, I was instantly relieved. Isaac and I had talked about traveling more, but had never made it a priority.

I looked down when he squeezed my hand. For some reason, that reassured me that everything really was okay. I knew his job could be stressful at times. I would've bet a million dollars that his recent strange behavior could be tied back to that culprit.

"Babe, I think I will take that drink," he said.

I squeezed his hand back and grinned even harder.

"Crown and cran, with a splash of lime?" I offered as I bopped over to the pantry.

"You know me so well."

It wasn't what he said that stopped me cold. It was the way he said it, and the way his voice trailed off into silence, that gave me a strange feeling. I didn't think he was looking for a response or reaction from me, but I found his comment really strange.

"Yes. Yes, Isaac, I do know you well; you are my husband," I joked.

When he didn't laugh or even chuckle, a quick thought flashed through my mind. Instantly, I scolded myself for entertaining it. Isaac had been a great husband and a man of strong character. There was no need for Sylvia to call her dog on my husband. Just as she'd discovered Jayden wasn't doing a thing wrong, I suspected the same about Isaac.

And why shouldn't I? He had never given me any reason to

think he'd step out on me, and I wholeheartedly believed that birds of a feather flocked together.

I welcomed Isaac and Jayden's friendship. I knew they had a lot in common. Sylvia and I had once heard the two boasting about grandiose accomplishments about women they'd dated in the past, but they were joking.

Being married for a number of years didn't cut me off from the real world in any way whatsoever. When it came to our men, Sylvia and I had two good ones.

After I fixed the drink, I placed it in front of Isaac and whispered in his ear, "I'm about to go and pick up some Chinese food for dinner."

"That'll work."

Isaac really liked Chinese food, so that was an easy decision to make.

Almost as if it was an afterthought, he quickly said, "Oh, you want me to go?"

Purse on shoulder and keys in hand, I dangled them for him to see. "I'll be back really fast."

CHAPTER TWENTY-ONE

Jayden

Sylvia had just come out of the house and briefly glanced at me before she opened her car door. I shut down the lawn-mower, removed my gardening gloves, and approached her.

"Baby, I'm going to visit my mom for a little while. She's having another one of her depressing pity parties, and she has once again manipulated me into coming over to spend time with her. I swear, it's times like this that I really wish I had a sibling," Sylvia griped as she tossed her purse on the passenger seat.

Sylvia and her mother had what I would classify as a dysfunctional relationship. They needed emotional drama to function.

"What's her crisis this time?" I asked out of a sense of marital politeness, but I was only mildly interested in her mother's affairs.

"She has relapsed into depression about my father divorcing her after thirty-two years. She feels as if she is not worthy of being loved. Now I have to go and remind her of how much I love and need her."

"Your parents have been divorced for five years. Why can't she just let it go? It seems like she is wearing bitterness like it's her favorite blanket."

"She's wounded, okay? There is nothing wrong with her feeling the way she does. Her entire life fell apart when my father left."

Sylvia furrowed her eyebrows. She was clearly offended by my lack of compassion. I also sensed that she harbored deep animosity toward her father as well.

"Have you talked to your old man lately?" I asked.

"No. I'm still mad at the bastard for leaving and breaking my mother's heart," Sylvia remarked as she positioned herself in the driver's seat.

"You should call him. I know that he's tried to contact you several times. No matter what, he's still your father. Give the guy some credit. Besides, five years is a long time to hold a grudge."

"Have you taken his side in all of this?" Sylvia directed her aggravation directly at me.

"It's not about choosing sides; it's about you creating a good relationship with the man." From time to time, I allowed my philosophical side to emerge when I thought it would be useful. "He didn't divorce you; he divorced unhappiness."

"Have you been talking to him? That sounds like something he would say." Sylvia's question was intertwined with a tone of betrayal.

"I'm still cool with the guy, and I know that he wants to have a better relationship with you, Sylvia. He's hurting and misses you guys more than he's willing to admit," I said. I reflected on the last time I had spoken to him. I had run into him at a nearby gas station. We chatted briefly, and when he mentioned Sylvia and how she wouldn't return his calls, I heard his voice tighten up.

"I refuse to talk to him right now. I'm not going to pretend to be his happy daughter. I believe that couples need to be mature and honest enough with each other to resolve their issues. Marriages would last much longer if men and women communicated openly like we do. Well, like we do most of the time," she said.

She fired up the motor. The radio came to life, and the smooth voice of Jill Scott flowed through the speaker system.

"Again, five years is a long time to hold on to your anger. If you don't let it go, it will take its toll." Sylvia remained silent. "Well, tell your mom hello for me." We leaned toward each other and kissed. When I pulled back, I felt as if I'd just kissed a plastic toy.

"When will you be back?" I asked.

"It will probably be later on this evening. In order to get her out of her self-pity parade, I'm going to take her furniture shopping with me. I want her opinion on a new bedroom set I'm interested in buying." Sylvia put the car in reverse.

"All right. I might go out and catch a movie later." I stepped away.

"Before you go, would you please replace the bar that my clothes are hanging on in the spare bedroom? I've pulled all of them off of the rack so you can do it."

"What about the rest of the stuff in there. Have you organized it yet?"

"No, I'll do it once the bar is replaced. I need to go through some of those clothes and donate them to Goodwill. You should donate that old, college trunk of yours that's at the back of that closet. It's bulky and it's just taking up space." Sylvia knew my college memorabilia was in the trunk, and awaited my reaction.

"I forgot all about that old trunk. I'll pull it out," I said.

"Don't spend all day going through it, Jayden. I think the only things inside it are old theater playbills and stage props. That part of your life is old news. You're a man now, and not some college boy." Sylvia smiled with condemnation and pulled away.

As I watched her drive away, I thought how I never liked her cutting comments. No matter how many times I tried to communicate the sentimental value of my memorabilia, Sylvia always insisted that I get rid of it. I didn't think it was silly or immature to hang on to that stuff. It represented a chapter in my life—the chapter that I had always longed to rewrite. If I could travel back in time, as the man I am today, I'd go to the night that changed the course of my existence and stop myself from doing something foolish. I would go back to the night that Sylvia's sensuality, opportunity, and my unbridled lust crossed paths. As I thought about it, I gazed around my yard and at my home. It represented the life that I had built on a foundation of shame. To outsiders, my house and life with Sylvia appeared admirable, but it wasn't. On the inside, it was spiritually cold, like a fish on a block of ice. Like her father, after decades of marital war and compromise, my diseased marriage had begun to show symptoms. I found myself caught in the crosshairs of either fixing it, or leaving it. It was a difficult choice that I needed to make. I exhaled, and gazed up at the puffy clouds which reminded me of a cluster of cotton balls. I recalled the day I'd made a life-altering decision.

Cheryl, Sylvia, and I had become friends. It was not uncommon for Sylvia to hang out with Cheryl and me when we would go on a date. Cheryl trusted Sylvia unconditionally and didn't mind her presence. I enjoyed having Sylvia around. It gave the perception that I was a young Casanova. It was an image that I happily embraced.

One day, Cheryl received news that her grandmother had suddenly become ill, and had to be hospitalized. The report she received was grim and she immediately left campus to be at her grandmother's side. I was sad, and felt horrible that I couldn't be with her. On that same day, Sylvia called me. She claimed to be upset about Cheryl's situation and didn't want to be alone. She asked if I wanted someone to keep me company. Without giving it much thought, I agreed and invited her over. Sylvia showed up at my dorm room dressed to kill. She had on a short, denim mini skirt and a hot pink shirt, with the collar flipped up and unbuttoned down to the valley of her breasts. As the thought of kissing her breasts entered my mind, I unconsciously swept my tongue across my lips like a dog who had just eaten a satisfying meal. I snapped myself out of my lustful thinking and looked into her deep chocolate eyes. I noticed that a flirtatious smile had formed on her face. She walked in and I shut the door. I turned and noticed the roundness of her ass in a way that I could not in the presence of Cheryl. An erection began to stir. I shoved my hands deep into the pockets of my sweat pants in an effort to conceal my hunger. My roommate wasn't there, so Sylvia made herself comfortable on my bed. She kicked off her shoes and positioned herself so that her back rested against the wall. I sat in a chair at my desk and tried unsuccessfully to conceal my excitement.

"Why are you playing?" she asked as she crossed one leg over the other.

"What do you mean?" I felt as if my manhood had developed Herculean strength and would rip through the thick cotton fabric of my sweatpants.

"You know what I'm talking about." I focused on her crimson lipstick and delicious lips. My eyes then traveled the length of her succulent thighs and shapely calves.

"No, I don't," I lied, and she knew it.

"What are you thinking about right now?" She twisted her finger around a strand of her hair.

"Nothing," I lied again. In truth, the only thought I had in my head was screwing her.

"Can I ask you a personal question?"

"Sure," I answered, thankful for the opportunity to focus on something other than sexual angst. I had hoped her question would have something to do with Cheryl's situation, but that wasn't the case.

"Cheryl told me that you guys haven't done it yet, and that you were okay with waiting until you were married. Is that really true?" Her question was bold and direct. Her gaze was locked on me. She studied my reaction for the truth. She was smart enough to not trust my answer.

After a long pause, I replied, "Yeah, that's what I said."

She chuckled and began rubbing her thighs. "Are you totally devoted to Cheryl?" Her questions felt like uncomfortable needle pricks.

"Of course I am." The way I shifted awkwardly in my seat didn't match the words that came out of my mouth.

"So, if I were to take off all of my clothes right now, and say that you could have sex with me instead of having to wait for Cheryl, you would tell me no?" She anxiously awaited my answer. I was momentarily paralyzed by opportunity. My ego kicked in, and I coolly leaned back in my chair. Her scenario triggered my deep yearning to lose my virginity.

"Yes," I uttered barely above a whisper.

"Liar!" she responded sharply.

"You're right. I am a liar." My eyes focused on her erect nipples which pushed out against the fabric of her shirt. She reached back, unbuttoned her skirt, and shimmied out of it. She had on purple panties that looked great against her chocolate skin.

"So, do you want to have sex right now, or do you want to wait for church-girl Cheryl?"

"Sylvia, I…" I stopped talking. I heard my ego tell me that I had arrived at the moment I had longed for. My lust pleaded with me not to ruin it. I forced myself not to overthink the situation, or to question Sylvia as to why she wanted to do this.

"Do you want to do this or not?" She removed her blouse, unclasped her bra, and freed her mouthwatering breasts. She got on her hands and knees and positioned herself at the foot of my bed. She slowly eased her face close to mine. I could smell the cool scent of peppermint on her breath.

"Sylvia," I whispered her name, but I did not recognize my own voice. My mind was completely focused on the moment and any thoughts or emotions about Cheryl vanished.

"Yes?" She moved in closer, and so did I. We paused at an invisible line, as if to give each other one final opportunity to change our minds. We didn't alter our course and kissed. Her lips were succulent and soft. Our tongues danced in circles in the cave of my mouth. I couldn't and didn't want to stop. I wanted to graduate into manhood and rid myself of virginity and the curse of inexperience. She encouraged me to join her on my bed. I removed my clothes and watched as she removed her purple panties and spread her thighs.

"Come on," she whispered sweetly. I positioned myself above her and she welcomed me into the soft, moist folds of her paradise.

The following month, Sylvia called me and delivered the news that her cycle was late.

CHAPTER TWENTY-TWO

Bailey

I t was as if my entire body had fallen off of Mount Everest. My heart took a drastic and sharp nosedive. I struggled to bring my eyes into focus. The fast flood of tears blurred my vision, but not so much that I couldn't see the truth.

Everything in my house was gone! The refrigerator, the stove, and even the custom cabinet doors were all gone. I stood with my mouth hung wide open, and stared back at my reflection. All that was left were the massive self-portraits that hung on the walls.

"What the fuc—" I couldn't even bring myself to finish the phrase. My leather sofas, the custom glass coffee table, the authentic African masks—absolutely everything had disappeared.

Although I could see the place was empty, I rushed from one room to the next. I suppose I hoped for a mirage effect. Maybe I was so tired, I was only imagining what my eyes had confirmed. "Michael! Miiichael," I cried.

Regardless of which room I rushed into, the results were still the same. Panic rushed through my veins. The guest bathroom was missing the toilet, along with the French handcrafted wooden armoire, and the large, life-sized mirror that had leaned against the wall.

I rushed back out to the living room and searched for my house phone. It was gone too. That's when I decided I needed to call someone. There was no way I'd be able to make it through this alone.

I grabbed my purse, and snatched the phone out. I quickly dialed the only number that came to mind.

"Hello?" Ava greeted.

At first, I could barely find my voice.

"Hello?" Ava called out again. Her voice grew louder, laced with concern.

"Bailey, what's wrong? Are you okay?"

"I...can't..." I began to sob.

"What?" Ava screamed into the phone. "What, Bailey? What can't you do?"

"Everything is gone. Everything, I don't understand," I stammered.

"Okay, Bailey, I need you to pull it together. I need you to calm down and tell me what the hell is going on. What do you mean, everything is gone? You're not making sense; put Michael on the phone," Ava instructed.

The mention of his name sent me into shock. I howled and crumpled to the floor. Had Michael done this to me? What had provoked this outrageous violation?

Ava's voice sounded like it was coming from a toy by the time I realized she was still on the phone. I did what little I could to try and pull myself together, but there was no use.

"Ava, sorry. I gotta go."

"Oh, no! What do you mean you gotta go? What's going on over there? Where's Michael, and what happened to your stuff?"

I heard her questions, but the words simply swam around in my head. I couldn't answer. I didn't know myself.

"I'm sorry, Ava," I repeated. "I gotta go. I need to call the police," I said.

As I talked to Ava, I pulled myself up from the floor and began to walk around the empty house. This time around, I could visualize everything that was missing. Who takes cabinet doors? When did someone have time to move all of this stuff, my stuff?

Ava didn't let up. She fired questions to me through the phone at such a rapid rate, my brain began to hurt. I felt overwhelmed.

I pressed a button and ended the call. My next call was to the police.

The moment the 9-1-1 dispatcher answered, I broke down again.

"Ma'am, are you in any danger?" the dispatcher asked.

"No, no; but all of my stuff is gone." I sobbed.

"I've already dispatched officers. They should be there in minutes. But if you are not in any immediate danger—"

"Please, stay on the phone with me. I can't take this. I don't understand what happened. What if someone hurt my boyfriend and they decide to come back for me?"

The loud knock on the door pulled my attention away from the dispatcher on the phone.

"Ma'am, those are the officers. Ms. Jones, I need you to open the door and let them in," she said.

I stumbled to the door and pulled it open. Once I saw the two uniformed officers, I ended the call and pulled the door wide enough for them to see.

"Someone has stolen everything out of my house and I don't know where my boyfriend is or whether he was kidnapped," I said.

As the words left my lips, I had an odd feeling. The officers must've sensed something. One of them turned to me and said, "Why would someone kidnap your boyfriend?"

His tone seemed to connect the dots for me.

"Michael did this to me?"

The officers looked at each other, then back at me. They had already pulled out their little notepads and began to write.

"Tell us about this boyfriend of yours, Michael," the officer said.

I suddenly felt like a naïve fool. Of course Michael hadn't been kidnapped. I pulled myself together as much as possible and cleared my throat.

After I gave the officers Michael's full name and description, I realized I really didn't know too much about him. I wanted a man so badly and thought I had found Mr. Right in a man I should never have trusted.

The signs were all there. He didn't work; he probably didn't have a place to live until I took him in. But I didn't want to accept the truth.

I led the officers around the house from room to room, explaining what was missing. It wasn't until we arrived back at the front room that one of them asked something I had never even considered.

"This building, isn't there security all around? Your neighbors or someone in the offices had to have seen something," he suggested.

Still sniffling and trying to hold it all together, I realized he was making good sense. That was one of the main reasons I enjoyed living in the building. A quiet moment was rare and I loved knowing that there was always a traffic flow.

"We're going down to talk to someone from management; you should come with us."

As we rode the elevator down, I thought about how long it had taken Michael to clean me out.

Heads turned and eyes gawked as I was escorted by the two officers. One of my neighbors, Katy Weiss, boldly asked if everything was okay.

"I thought you had moved," she said.

The officers stopped and looked at her.

"Ma'am, did you see anything?" one of them asked.

"Oh, yes. I was working from home today when I saw about a dozen moving men going in and out of Bailey's place. I mentioned to my husband that I didn't know she was moving, and wondered why she hadn't said so."

"Why did you think these were moving men?"

"Oh, well, they all had on those dreadful work uniforms. You know, those large, one-piece coveralls," Katy said. Her features were twisted with visible worry and concern.

She clutched her pearls. "Oh, my, don't tell me you've been robbed," she declared. Horror quickly spread across her face.

"Ma'am, I'm going to ask you a few more questions if you don't mind. Ms. Jones is going to speak with my partner and property management."

The officer's partner nudged me slightly in the direction of the leasing office. But the moment I turned, I nearly bumped right into a visibly panic-stricken Ava.

"Sweet Jesus, Bailey! What in the hell is going on with you?" She rushed a trembling hand to her lips once her eyes connected with the officer at my side.

CHAPTER TWENTY-THREE

Ava

"I am too through with all this drama behind that airhead friend of yours," Sylvia snarled. "She gives all us women a bad name if you ask me."

Sylvia picked up her Martini glass by the stem and carefully brought it to her lips.

All I could do was shake my head at the foolishness myself. I didn't approve of the choices Bailey made. As a matter-of-fact, I felt like those bad choices impacted our friendship quite a bit. But I wasn't about to be constantly hating on the poor chile. Besides, she was already down; kicking her now wouldn't help one bit.

"It's like her entire life is a mess and a half!" Sylvia added, with a dramatic eye roll.

We were supposed to be dishing over expensive appetizers and cheap cocktails. Usually, Sylvia and I enjoyed happy hour. In the midst of the bustling restaurant crowd, we'd people-watch, talk about our husband's shortcomings, or bitch and moan about work. Here lately, I had intentionally kept Bailey out of our conversations, especially since prior to two days ago, I hadn't heard from her for nearly two weeks.

Originally, when I agreed to happy hour with Sylvia, the plan was to take her up on the offer to put her private investigator to work on Michael. But who knew the way things were going to unfold over the last few days.

"Yeah, I feel kinda bad for her, though," I said.

Sylvia sucked her teeth and frowned a bit. "Well, I don't feel sorry for that heifer one bit. You tried to tell her that fool couldn't be trusted, but some women are so stupidly dick-whipped, they can't even come up for air, let alone think straight!"

"Ouch!"

Sylvia looked at me, but her features hadn't softened one bit. "Ava, get real!" Her neck snaked. "You can't expect me to feel sorry for some nitwit who treated you like crap just because you tried to warn her to be careful. Remember, she accused you of being jealous or some foolishness like that." Sylvia swatted her words away with a dismissive hand. "Next topic," she added.

I didn't say anything as she took a sip of her drink. I hated when I felt torn between my two closest friends. Yes, there was no question about it, Bailey had her issues. She was far from perfect, but weren't we all to a certain extent?

Sylvia certainly wasn't perfect either, and I was sure she knew it. But the way she came down on Bailey made me suddenly glad I hadn't brought up the topic of using her private investigator to look into Michael after all.

"Seriously, though, you need to cut ties with that dingbat," Sylvia said as she stuffed a Shrimp Brochette into her mouth.

"I've known Bailey since we were kids," I defended.

"That doesn't mean a damn thing. So what, just because you've known her since you were a kid, that means you have to stress yourself with her self-inflicted problems? I mean, I don't know her personally, but from what you've told me, she bounces through life making one poor choice after another. Then she has the nerve to wonder why she can't seem to get ahead." Sylvia shook her head in exasperation. "Besides, you ever heard of outgrowing some-one?" Her thin, brown eyebrows dipped into a concentrated frown. "It's not a crime, and it happens all the time." She shrugged.

"Yeah, I hear you, but I'm also sure it's not easy being single these days," I said.

I knew Sylvia would think I was defending Bailey and to an extent, I guess I was. But I knew for a fact that Bailey wasn't some dumb airhead. She was very well-respected in corporate circles, and she was educated with a MBA. I had no idea why she made such poor choices when it came to men and her personal life, but to me, everyone had their weaknesses.

"So what happened when the office manager said they weren't liable?"

I shrugged. I took a sip of my martini and sighed. "The police took a report and asked for a picture of Michael. I can't imagine that they're gonna find his butt."

"See, that's a damn shame. She meets some guy; he's unem-ployed, but still, less than thirty days later, she moves him into her place and suddenly she's shocked when he rips her off?" Sylvia said with a sharp laugh. "Raise your hand if you didn't see this one ending in total disaster."

I rolled my eyes, and then began to look around the restaurant. I was ready to go. The whole beat-up-on-Bailey-during-happy-hour had taken all of the happy out of the evening for me.

"What's wrong with you?" Sylvia looked up and asked.

"Nothing. I'm ready to go," I said somberly.

"Oh, why? We ain't even had two rounds yet."

"I know, but I need to get to the house. I still need to figure out what to fix for Isaac," I lied.

Sylvia gave me a sideways glance that told me she wasn't buying my story for a second, but I didn't care. I knew Bailey needed to make better choices. Still there was a part of me that couldn't help but feel for her after what had happened. I wished she'd find somebody who really wanted what she wanted.

As I drove home after drinks with Sylvia, I thought about how fortunate we were. I'd read in an issue of *Essence* magazine that the number of single, black women was some unprecedented number, and while some of those women were probably happily single, I could only imagine the number of them who were in the same boat as Bailey. They hated being single, and every man they encountered reminded them of just how alone and lonely they were.

Despite my husband's issues, I was so glad I wasn't out there doing the dating thing. When you had that many single, desperate women, it might as well be a free-for-all for men.

I didn't think anything of the fact that I'd pulled into our driveway, and Isaac's car wasn't there yet. My mind and heart were heavy with thoughts of Bailey and her newest set of issues.

"Wait 'til I tell Isaac about this one," I muttered as I got out of the car. It wasn't until I was inside our bedroom and about to take a shower that I realized my husband sure had been working late a lot lately.

"Girl, please, don't let your friend's man issues become yours. You know good and well you got yourself a damn good man!"

Before I changed my clothes, I grabbed the phone and dialed Isaac's cell.

After a few seconds, I cocked my head, puzzled, at the sound of his voicemail that came on after the first ring.

"Hmm. What's his cell phone doing off and he's not home?"

I looked at the phone as if it might have malfunctioned and dialed my husband's number again.

I was baffled when I got the exact same result.

CHAPTER TWENTY-FOUR

Jayden

I sat on the sofa and massaged Sylvia's feet while we watched an episode of *Scandal*, a TV series we had both become hooked on.

"Oh, yes, right there; squeeze harder." Sylvia held her breath while my fingers worked their magic. "That feels so damn good," she cooed.

"I'm glad that I'm doing it to your satisfaction." I was happy that we were both in decent moods. When I finished rubbing her feet, Sylvia repositioned herself and snuggled up to me. We put our feet up on the oversized, leather ottoman and enjoyed our moment of tranquility.

"What are you thinking about?" Sylvia relaxed her body even more.

"About the conference in Philadelphia that I have to go to next week."

"Oh, thanks for reminding me. I had forgotten that you'll be gone for a few days."

"I would have reminded you." I inhaled deeply before slowly releasing my breath.

"Jayden," Sylvia murmured my name.

"Yes?"

"Do you regret marrying me?" I had not anticipated that question and I didn't relish the idea of engaging in a difficult conversation. I was never good at, nor did I have, strong confrontation skills.

"Why are you asking a question like that?" If there was one thing I learned about Sylvia over the years, there was always a reason behind questions that came seemingly hurdling out of nowhere.

"Ever since Greg left, something has been off with us. You've been distant with me. If I have done something to make you mad or upset with me, please let me know." Sylvia repositioned herself so that she could look into my eyes. She wanted to read my facial expressions.

I felt my chest tighten, so I growled to clear it and used that as a temporary distraction. In my mind, I debated on whether or not to tell her the painful truth or tell her nothing was bothering me so that our evening wouldn't turn sour.

"I think I'm going through a mid-life thing." I elected to be truthful in a gentle way.

"Are you not happy with me and our life?" She asked another probing question that kicked me in the gut.

"Lately I've been asking myself whether or not my life and yours would be different had our son not played a role in our choosing to get married." This time, I waited and anticipated an explosive and emotional response. Unpredictably, Sylvia was calm and didn't come back with a cutting remark.

"Is that why you searched the Internet and found Cheryl? Do you want to be with her?"

"No, I don't want to be with her. I was just curious as to what she was up to. I have not made any type of contact, if that's what you're worried about," I said.

"Jayden, I need to feel safe and comfortable with you. I've noticed that ever since Bo sniffed out that old photo, you've been trickling down memory lane an awful lot. Is there something more I should know?"

"Just because I like being a little nostalgic doesn't mean that I have some hidden agenda." My expression hardened more than I wanted.

"I don't think that it's healthy to keep backsliding the way that you've been doing." Sylvia took my hand into her own. The genuineness of her touch made me feel at ease.

"Sylvia, they're just memories that I like entertaining from time to time," I said, confident I had allayed her suspicions.

"Okay, baby." She allowed the conversation to die and snuggled close to me again. I gave her a squeeze and the standard obligatory kiss that I had been giving for her decades.

"I meant to ask you, how did it go with your mom?"

"It's funny you should ask. She has finally gone to therapy like I suggested."

"Wow. I didn't know she needed that type of help," I said.

"Yeah, after hearing her complain about the same things over and over, I realized that she'd gotten stuck in a valley of despair and didn't know how to get out. Ava gave me a recommendation for her. The last time I talked to my mother, she admitted something that she had to face in her therapy sessions."

"What did she have to face?" Sylvia now had my full attention.

"The fact that she drove my father away."

"Huh?" I was stunned.

"Yeah. That came out in the therapy session. Over the years of their marriage, she was so afraid of him leaving her that she purposely sabotaged the trust in her marriage." Sylvia uncharacteristically took in a deep breath and let it out slowly, as if unburdening herself of a heavy weight.

"Are you okay?" I asked, drawing her closer.

"Yes. I just remembered my father always complaining about mother and her ways. Now I know why."

"So is that the real reason why he left? He knew that your mom was pushing him away," I said as more of a fact than a question.

"It looks that way."

"Babe, you should not have allowed your imagination to fill in the blanks about why your dad left. You should really talk to him. I know he would love to hear from you." I encouraged her the best way I knew how. Then I paused, thinking about how I could so easily try to fix her wounded heart, but struggled when it came to dealing with my own aches.

"I will. I'll call him first thing in the morning," Sylvia agreed.

"Good; you'll feel better when you do."

"You know, my mother said that she knew my father was a forward-thinking man, and that she was his opposite. She lived in the past a lot. While I was growing up, she always talked about how much fun she'd had when she was a little girl. She loved being with her dad. When my grandfather walked out, it left a big hole in her heart. She had never forgiven him for it and held on to antipathy. It was easier and didn't require strength the way forgiveness does. When my grandfather passed away, it wounded her soul horribly. She never forgave him. She regretted not letting him know how much she missed and needed him. The therapist told her that it was time to let go of the emotional baggage she'd been carrying around for decades."

"She needs to also forgive herself, if she hasn't done so yet." There was a long pause. "I never knew your mom was that wounded. I never got that type of vibe from her," I said.

"She was good at hiding it. Anyway, now that she's found the courage to deal with her unresolved issues, I've become her unofficial sounding board, and it has been challenging for me to deal with alone," she spoke softly.

"Why didn't you talk to me about this sooner?" I asked.

"You seemed more interested in old history rather than current events, and in my head, I intertwined your nostalgic behavior with my mother's. I went on a crusade of sorts to bring you into the present moment so that I could have your support. But I also feared that you didn't want me anymore and that upset me." I didn't expect Sylvia's honesty to hit me the way that it did. The depth of her love for me was more than I imagined. In that moment, I tried to abandon all thoughts and ideas of exiting my marriage, but I couldn't get them to leave and that bothered me.

The following morning, I got up and went for my morning run as always. When I returned to the house, I took a quick shower, and changed into a comfortable pair of shorts, a T-shirt, and sneakers. I had packed some items that I had meant to forward to Greg weeks ago. I decided to take his package to the post office and ship it to him. When I got to there, I noticed a woman standing beside her vehicle. She had a flat tire. I didn't say anything to her as I entered the post office. I figured she had AAA or some other roadside service she could call. I took care of mailing the package and walked back out. I found the woman on her hands and knees, trying to figure out how to jack up her vehicle.

"Are you okay?" I politely asked.

"No," she said as she steadied herself and rose back to her feet. "Do you know how this thing works?" She held up the car jack.

"Yeah, I do." I took it from her and positioned it properly beneath the car. "I take it that you don't have a service coming to help you."

"I do, but I am running really late for an important meeting and it's going to be at least two hours before someone gets to me." She let loose an agitated growl. "I do not need this shit today."

"Is your spare tire any good?"

"I have no clue. I don't ever look back there," the woman snapped.

"Let's take a look." I walked to the rear of the car, removed the covering, and unlatched the spare. I pulled it out and saw that it appeared to be fine.

"Looks like you have a fine spare here. I'll put the tire on for you so that you can be on your way."

"Would you really? Thank you so much. Here, let me give you some money." The woman opened her purse.

"You don't need to do that." I began to change her tire. Once I was done, I showed her a nail that she had run over which was the cause of the flat. I put the bad tire in the trunk and told her to have a great day.

"You're so kind," she said.

I smiled at her and walked away. I felt good about helping the woman out.

The following Monday, after I had gone through airport security, I went and got myself an espresso. Drink in hand, I walked down to my gate and took a seat. As I enjoyed my beverage, I decided to look over the notes I had written on my iPad. Around that time, a pair of long, mahogany legs strutted past me. The woman's legs were shapely, and it was obvious that she worked out. I inconspicuously allowed my eyes to travel upward over the smooth curvature of the calves and thighs. She was wearing a black, pin-striped pencil skirt and a light-blue, French-cuffed poplin shirt. She sat down and gazed at me. I didn't acknowledge the look, and didn't want her to know that I enjoyed looking at her body.

"This is just too coincidental." I looked up and the woman with the shapely legs stood before me.

"Excuse me?" I smiled.

"You don't remember me?" she asked. I searched my mind, but could not place her.

"Of course you wouldn't. I didn't even give you my name." She shifted her weight from one leg to the other. I quickly glanced at her hot legs again and tried not to let my hunger show.

"I'm sorry, but I just don't remember you." I hoped she would go back to where she had come from, and leave me with my thoughts and sensual imagination.

"My name is Bailey." She extended her hand, and I shook it.

"Jayden," I said and wondered why she seemed interested in me.

"You helped me at the post office last week when I had a flat tire." She made the connection that I couldn't.

"Oh, yeah, now I remember." I smiled again.

"Because of you, I made it to my meeting on time, and was able to close a big deal for my company," she explained.

"Well, I'm glad it all worked out."

"Are you on this flight to Philadelphia?"

"Yeah," I said and sat up a little straighter.

"So am I." She sat in the empty seat next to me to converse.

CHAPTER TWENTY-FIVE

Bailey

W hen the driver pulled up in front of my luxury hotel in the heart of Philadelphia's Center City, I couldn't help but beam with pride. I felt fabulous. I had closed a second huge deal that would bring even more business to my company.

A white-gloved hand opened the back door of the town car, moments after it pulled to a complete stop. I latched on to the other hand that was extended to me, and eased out of the back seat as gracefully as possible in my tight, pencil skirt. Red was my power color and it had worked wonders for me.

"Welcome to the Ritz-Carlton, Philadelphia, ma'am," the doorman greeted.

"Thank you," I said, as I walked through the doors and into the hotel's crisp air. The lobby's marble floors and massive columns hinted at the city's rich history, with just enough modern touches scattered throughout. I took in the plush sofas and contemporary chairs as the concierge approached me with a warm smile.

He was a tall, middle-aged man who looked to be of Middle Eastern descent. He wore a well-tailored business suit, and was clean-cut. "Ms. Jones. Good evening. How was your day?" he asked.

I was more than a little impressed that he had remembered my name.

"Oh, it was great! Thanks for asking."

"Wonderful. Is there something I can help you with this evening?"

"Yes. I want to know if there's someplace where I can have colleagues come in to sign some paperwork. I'm not sure if we'll require food or drinks, but I want them to be comfortable. To my knowledge, we are simply signing a few legal documents."

"Hmm." He motioned for me to follow him back to his desk. "Come, let me see what's available." He glanced back at me and asked, "Do you prefer to remain on-site? Or—"

"Yes, please, something right here at the hotel. I thought the bar would be too loud, but I don't want to be inside a large meeting room. Do you have anything in between? I'm expecting about six to eight people, including myself."

"I have the perfect place," he said, and started to bang on his keyboard. "Let me just make sure it is available. What time will your guests arrive?"

"They will be here at eight o'clock sharp. I think we should be able to take care of everything within about forty-five minutes, tops."

I watched as he squinted his hazel-green eyes at the monitor. Suddenly, he stopped, reached into his jacket pocket, and removed a small pair of reading glasses.

"Okay. Let's see here. We've got a small meeting room, which seats twelve. That should be enough space if you need to stretch out a bit."

"Perfect!" I said.

I waited as he made arrangements for me to have the small meeting room from eight to nine in the evening. Everything was falling perfectly into place and I couldn't be happier.

"Oh, one other thing, I'd like to arrange for a massage in my room, in about thirty minutes," I said.

"Let me check the availability. It's five-fifteen o'clock now. Oh, I see she's got an opening for six. Would you like me to book that for you?"

"Yes. That would be great. Thanks."

As I finished up there, I grabbed my bag and headed for the elevator.

"Hold the door!" I yelled and jogged to catch one that was just about to leave. A brown hand caught the door.

"We've gotta stop meeting like this!" Jayden said, as I rushed inside.

"Thanks for holding the doors," I said, trying not to sound so out of breath.

"You must've been really busy. I haven't seen you since we checked in the other day." He dragged his eyes up my body, took in my red pencil skirt, the crisp, white button-down shirt, and stopped at my ruby-red-hued lips.

"Oh, yes! I just closed a major deal. We're signing the papers this evening, and then I'm ready to celebrate," I boasted. I snapped my fingers and wiggled my hips a little.

"Uh-oh. These Philly brothas better watch out now!"

I stopped and rolled my eyes at him playfully. "Umm. By celebrate, I mean a drink at the bar after nine, once those contracts are signed and my colleagues are finally out of my hair for good," I added with a wink and a chuckle.

Jayden's face twisted into mock confusion. "What kind of celebration is that?" he asked. "That ain't no way to celebrate in the City of Brotherly Love."

"Maybe not for you," I pointed in his direction, then back at myself, "but you said so yourself, I've been swamped since we landed. I am looking forward to a quiet evening at the bar, even if the only company I have is the bartender. And I don't want to hear too much from him, I simply want him to keep the Rémy Martin Black Pearl flowing," I said.

"Damn! Okay, then. Well, I plan to go paint the town tonight. Before I head back, I'm gonna get it in. Come Sunday morning, I wanna be crawling back onto the plane," Jayden said.

The elevator ding came just in time. I came this close to telling his ol' tired behind he needed to go check in with his wife and stop chasing trouble, but that was her problem not mine. I kept my thoughts to myself.

"Oh, that's me. Well, Jayden, enjoy your night and don't hurt nobody out there."

"I can't make any promises," he joked.

I did a three-finger wave over my shoulder as I sauntered out of the elevator and down the hall.

"You sure you don't wanna come out with my friends and me tonight?" he yelled after me.

I kept it moving.

"I'm sure, but thanks for the invite. Be good!" I turned and went in the direction opposite my room. When I heard the elevator doors close, I pivoted, and rushed to the left. I didn't need any strange men knowing which room I was in.

Still on a natural high after closing the deal, I walked into my room and stripped immediately. I sat on the bed in my bra, panties, and pumps and ordered room service. Once that was done, I decided to shower before my masseuse was set to arrive.

It had been nearly one month since Michael had flipped my world upside down. The police were no closer to finding him, and as my life slowly began to take its familiar shape again, I felt good about all of the great things that were happening with work. Thank God I'd been so busy. I didn't have time to sit and feel sorry for myself.

I had used one of the company's interior designers, and she got my place back and comfortable in less than a week. Trying to look for the silver lining after what had happened, I told myself that the new makeover was well overdue anyway.

As I walked into the spacious bathroom in my suite, I decided to focus on only the positive. I loved hotel bathrooms. I turned on the shower and looked around. The Ritz's butterscotch-and-chocolate color scheme put me into a relaxed frame of mind. As steam began to fill the room, I reminded myself that I didn't have all day.

"Shoot, my massage is in less than twenty minutes!" I stepped into the shower, washed quickly, and got out. I hummed a Joss Stone tune as I dried and moisturized my body. Once finished, I pulled the robe from the hook on the back of the door, and walked back into the room.

It felt like I had just tightened the big fluffy white robe's band around my waist, when a booming knock sounded at the door.

"Man!" I grumbled as I rushed to the peephole. "That was quick."

CHAPTER TWENTY-SIX

Ava

"What time did you get in last night?" I pushed away the heavy feeling in my heart and poured Isaac a cup of coffee. I had been up for nearly an hour before I heard him make his way down the stairs and into our kitchen. I held the cup and placed it in front of him. When he acted like he didn't hear my question, I started to fume. Struggling to hold my feelings inside, I eased into a chair across from him and waited on an answer.

"You put any sugar in this? We out of that French Vanilla stuff?" he asked.

I got up from the chair and walked into the oversized pantry. Was this man losing his mind, or what? I wasn't trying to fight with him, but I'd be damned if I'd let him coast in and out of our house like he had no one to answer to.

There was only one sleeve left of the flavored creamer that he asked about, so I removed it from the box. I tossed the empty box into the garbage.

He eyed me as I took my time bringing it back to the table.

I held it out as if I was about to give it to him, then when he reached for it, I pulled it back.

Isaac wrinkled his eyebrows and focused his stare on me. The maroon-colored walls felt like they were closing in on us before my husband spoke.

"Woman! You think I'm in the mood to play with you?"

"I don't know. You've had so many mood swings lately, I never know who's showing up these days," I said.

His eyes fell to the thin packet I held between my thumb and index finger. I could read his thoughts before he tried his sneak move. He pulled his hand back and gave up, defeated when he didn't succeed.

"What's a man gotta do to get a decent cup of coffee around here?" He sighed, loud and hard.

"Answer his wife's question maybe?" I suggested, with a half shrug.

"Ava, what? What's with all the damn questions lately? Don't you have some friends whose lives need dissecting or something?"

His tone was nasty and cold. I took the thin packet into my hand, pulled the top of my robe open and eased it in next to my breast. My husband's expression hardened instantly. Suddenly, air in the room seemed to evaporate. The silence that hung between us seemed thicker than clam chowder and very uncomfortable.

"Come and get it if you really want it," I teased, in hopes of lightening the mood.

But my lighthearted attempt at humor seemed lost on him. The dark and cold expression that stared back at me nearly chilled me to the core.

Isaac shrugged and shook his head slowly. "Just a cup of coffee, that's all I want. I'd like to sit here and enjoy a quiet cup of coffee. Is that too much to ask?" He threw his hands up in defeat.

"What time did you come in last night?" I asked again.

A few beats passed between us. But I refused to relent.

Moments later, still nothing.

"Okay. Okay. It was late. There, you happy? Now, can I get the stuff for the coffee, please?"

I reluctantly pulled the packet out of my top and slid it across the table. I watched as he ripped it open, and dumped the contents into his coffee mug. He used his finger to stir it in. He took a sip and closed his eyes as if he was in heaven. I waited.

"Something is not right," I said.

Isaac looked at me. "Don't try to make something out of nothing. I lost track of the time and came in kinda late. Nothing to get all hot and bothered about."

I knew in my heart of hearts that this was not a battle I wanted. But I also knew that my husband had been acting strange lately, and I wanted to get to the bottom of what was bothering him.

"How long have I been married to you?" I asked. My goal was to try a different approach. Joking with him seemed like a waste of time, so I waited for his answer.

When he rolled his eyes and took a palm to slap his forehead, I was crushed. How could such a simple conversation frustrate him so?

"Ava. Why do you insist on creating a situation where one does not exist? I told you, there are lots of changes at work. I'm trying to deal with them. It's that simple. There's nothing wrong; there's nothing out of the ordinary. But yet, you wanna act like the world is coming to an end. I've been married to you long enough to know your pattern. And, Ava, I'm trying to tell you, don't go looking for problems when there ain't none to find."

"All you had to say was work. All that other crap wasn't even necessary," I said. I got up from the chair and walked out of the kitchen.

Isaac and his mood swings had worked my very last, damn nerve. If he wanted to let work stress him out to the point where he looked like he had aged overnight, then so be it. I was done. I could find better things to occupy my time.

I went up to our bedroom, changed my clothes, and combed

my hair. It was a gorgeous San Diego Saturday. I was not about to sit up in the house with a miserable man.

Since Bailey was out of town, I couldn't stop in on her, and I wasn't sure I wanted to be around Sylvia's sarcastic behind either.

I grabbed my purse and keys and walked toward the front door. Isaac must've caught a glimpse of me. He pulled himself from wherever his imagination had him and asked, "Going out?"

"Yup," was all I said, as I walked out of the house.

You didn't have to tell me twice. If he wanted to act like an asshole and dump all over people, he'd have to find someone else. I wasn't in the mood either.

"Maybe I'll go have lunch on the Pier or something like that," I said to myself as I got into my car.

As I turned the ignition, the phone rang. It was Sylvia.

"Hey, lady," she greeted.

She sounded cheerful and that caught me a little off-guard. I hadn't talked to her much since we had gone for drinks and she had pissed me off. At work it was easy to avoid private conversation since we were always busy.

"Hey, what's going on?" I asked unenthusiastically.

"Girl, not a damn thing. You know Jayden is out of town, and with Greg gone, sometimes I struggle with being alone," she said.

It was strange to me how I could relate to what she was saying and I hadn't experienced nearly half of the life changes she had gone through.

"What are you doing?" she asked.

"Oh, about to find an outlet mall to go to for a few hours."

Sylvia grunted a bit. She absolutely hated outlet shopping. Usually, just the mention of one sent her off on a tirade about how expensive they were, and how much false advertising worked on the rest of us fools who got sucked into going.

"Uh, you mind if I tag along?" she asked.

"You want to go, umm, to the outlets with me?" I asked again. It was more to make sure she had understood where I said I was going.

"Yeah, I want to pick up something nice for Jayden before he gets back tomorrow," she nearly sang.

Now it was my turn to wonder whether it was me, and not the people around me, who had been behaving strangely.

CHAPTER TWENTY-SEVEN

Jayden

Early Saturday evening, I was in my hotel room getting ready to head out to a Philadelphia 76ers game. The convention organizers had given me tickets as a gift for being a presenter at their conference. I had two tickets, but would only be able to use one of them. I figured I would brighten someone's day by giving it away.

Before I left, I decided to call Sylvia and check in. I would be getting back to my hotel room late and wouldn't feel like talking after the game. When I called, she didn't answer. I sent her a text message and she responded, saying that she was out with Ava and couldn't talk. I knew that they were probably talking about Isaac. Before I left, he had mentioned that he sensed Ava's intuition had kicked in, and she had become suspicious. Since I knew that Ava wasn't around him, I decided to give him a buzz.

"What's up, man?" I greeted him.

"Bullshit."

"Damn, playa, it's like that?" I stood in front of the bathroom mirror. I turned on the faucet so that I could give myself a quick shave.

"Man, you won't believe what this chick has done."

"We're talking about your sidepiece, right?" I wanted to be certain.

"Yeah."

"What happened? Don't tell me you got arrested again," I asked.

"Nah, man, she's trying to get child support before the baby even gets here. She went down to the damn Public Assistance office and gave the bastards my name." I heard a tornado of emotions in Isaac's voice.

"Get the fuck out? Really?" I was stunned, although after thinking for a moment, realized that Isaac had to have known that he would have to pay child support.

"Man, you know once the government gets in your ass they stay a while. I'm going to have to learn how to shit differently once they're done. The damn Public Assistance office sent some paperwork work to the house. I was glad that I got to the mailbox before Ava did. She would have opened the shit up, and I would have gotten busted."

"How did they get your address, and when are you going to tell Ava?" I asked. I wanted to push him into revealing what was going on so that it would lighten the load of the secret he was carrying.

"I don't know how she got my address. And I was hoping to never tell her."

"That's not realistic, man. As hard as it's going to be, you're going to have to face the issue." I sat the phone down and placed it on speaker as I lathered up my face and began to shave.

"I just don't know how Ava is going to take this mess I've gotten into. I feel like a kite caught in a hurricane. I don't know which way the damned wind is going to blow me."

"I can only imagine how hard it is for you right now. As far as how Ava is going to take the news, well, you know that she's going to be pissed off. She'll probably feel betrayed, lied to, and hurt. You might as well prepare yourself for some difficult days," I spoke truthfully.

"You ain't helping me, Jayden," Isaac raised his voice at me.

"I'm telling you what you need to hear and not what you want to hear. Man, you've gotten yourself into some real shit here."

"Tell me what I want to hear; it sounds better," Isaac said.

"Nah, I can't do that. I wouldn't be a true friend if I did."

"Okay, if you had gotten your ass in a situation like this, how would you handle it?"

"You really want me to tell you how to handle it?" I asked.

"Forget it, man. You're mocking me and you probably don't know shit anyway."

I knew Isaac didn't mean what he said. I understood that he was angry with himself. The mess he had gotten himself into had rocked his world, and he was reacting emotionally to a very difficult situation.

"Hey, do you want my suggestion or not?"

He was silent for a moment. "Yeah, what do you suggest?"

"Okay, I don't remember where I heard this from or why I remember it, but here goes. When you tell Ava that you've messed up, she's going to be super pissed, so you have to anticipate that. In fact, before you tell her, make sure everything that you want to keep intact is out of the house."

"Okay, I like what you're saying so far." Isaac listened attentively.

"When you make the announcement say, 'Baby, I am a low-down bastard, and you deserve a better man than me. I know you can't stand to be around me right now, and I don't blame you. I can't even look at myself. I've packed up my shit already and I'm leaving.' Then make sure you have a hotel room or if money is tight, head over to your parents' house and chill. Eventually, after she's done talking badly about you to Sylvia and calms down, she'll realize that she's in that house all alone, and she'll hate that feeling. That's when she'll start thinking really hard, and wondering how the marriage ended up where it is. That's also when she'll want to talk about it rationally. At that point, you need to be honest with her, and tell her how you got involved with Denise. Tell her the type of affair it was, and the ways in which you were pushed into the arms of another woman. You're going to have to do some soul searching to find the truth as to why you did what you did."

"Jayden, that's the dumbest shit I've ever heard."

"No, what's crazy is yo' ass screwing around without a condom. Real talk, man, there is a lot of temptation out there. Even the best among us can be seduced."

Isaac was silent, and then laughed painfully.

"Put your big daddy drawers on, and do what you've got to do," I said.

"Yeah, man, you're right. I've got to face this at some point." Isaac held on to his words for a long moment and then changed the subject. "Are you still in Philly?"

"Yeah, I'm going to a 76ers game tonight," I explained as I took a face towel, wet it with warm water, and removed the excess shaving cream.

"Are you staying out of trouble?" he asked.

"Yeah, Sylvia and I talked a few days ago about our relationship. We are just in an okay place. She wants the relationship a bit more than I do. At least that's the way I feel at the moment."

"You're just as conflicted as I am." Isaac exhaled. "Well, enjoy the game, and don't try to hook up with a cheerleader. They'll drain you to the bone."

"Ha, I'd show those young twenty-year-olds what a grown man can do." I laughed and then snapped my fingers. "Dude, I meant to tell you about this chick I met on my flight out here."

"Okay, you scold me about getting involved with Denise, and now you want to switch up and tell me about a chick you met on your flight?"

"I know. It sounds bad, but I'm just saying, I met this lady."

"Don't go and fuck up like I have, Jayden," Isaac said.

"Man, please. I'm the one who taught you the fine art of behaving badly when you're away from home. Just like every woman has a good and bad girl inside her, every guy has a husband and a playboy side. Anyway, she's some type of corporate real estate executive and she is so doable, if you know what I mean."

"I understand. Have you hooked up with her yet?"

"Nah, I'm not even sure if she's still in town. I was hoping to run into her at the bar last night, but I got back too late."

"So why are you telling me about a chick you don't really even know?"

"Hell, I am hoping to have a sexually indulgent encounter while here. Nothing serious, just casual and protected sex."

"Well, make sure your ass has double coverage, if you know what I mean," Isaac said.

"I know what you mean. Listen, if you need anything, let me know. I imagine that you're going through hell right now and it's not pretty."

"Thanks, Jayden," Isaac muttered. "I'll talk to you later. I have to think about how and when I'm going to tell Ava."

"Okay."

"Yeah," Isaac whispered and then hung up.

I continued to get dressed. I put on my jeans, a nice polo shirt, and sprayed on some Calvin Klein cologne. I grabbed my tickets and exited my hotel room. When I got down to the lobby, I asked the doorman to hail me a cab.

"It will be a few minutes, sir. There is a line in front of you," he said as he exited the building and blew his whistle.

I saw where the line of people had formed and awaited my turn. I noticed a yellow cab pull up. The doorman opened the door and when I saw a pair of shapely legs emerge from the cab, I knew that it was Bailey. She was carrying multiple shopping bags and had on dark sunglasses. As she moved past me, I leaned in and got her attention.

"Is there a thank-you gift for changing your flat tire in one of those bags?" I jokingly asked.

"Oh my God, you startled me," Bailey said as she looked in my direction.

"I apologize." I held up my hands.

"Yeah," she said, quick and sharp as if she were determining whether or not to be bothered with me. "Now what did you just ask me?"

"If there was a gift in one of your bags for me."

Bailey frowned. "Honey, I tried to pay you twice."

I was puzzled. "No, you only tried to pay me once."

"Men, I swear, everything has to be explained." She headed inside. I stepped out of line and grabbed one of her bags for her.

"Come on, I will walk with you into the lobby so that you can explain what I've missed." Bailey stopped and studied me. She turned slowly away and wiggled her hips a little as she walked.

"I had hoped you'd come down to the bar last night. I thought I dropped a big enough hint," she explained.

"I would have loved to, but unfortunately I was out very late." I licked my lips. I was hoping to have a little luck. I was sexually attracted to her and wanted to have some fun.

"I see. Well, I plan on enjoying a cocktail. Why don't you join me?" she suggested.

"Are you asking me out on a date?" I asked jokingly.

She pushed her sunglasses down to the tip of her nose. "Sitting at a hotel bar is hardly a date."

"I've got a better idea. I have an extra ticket to the 76ers game. Why don't you join me?"

"Now *that* would be a date. I don't even know you and you expect me to…" Bailey paused. She looked me up and down and judged me. "What would your wife say if she knew you were out of town horsing around?"

I laughed as I felt the devil rise in me. "What my wife doesn't know won't hurt her. Besides, I'm just looking to have a fun time at the game. If you're not comfortable with that, I understand." There was an awkward moment of silence that hung in the air like the quiet that lingers after an explosion. Bailey pursed her lips.

"What the hell. Your wife is your business, not mine. Besides, I ain't doing shit anyway," she said. "Can you give me thirty minutes to freshen up?"

"Absolutely." I gave her bag back to her and watched as she wiggled away toward the elevators. I found a seat and waited with anticipation, like a child eager to unwrap holiday gifts.

CHAPTER TWENTY-EIGHT

Bailey

The atmosphere inside the Wells Fargo Center was already lively before the game even started. As we made our way to our seats, I took in the banners that hung from the rafters that displayed the retired numbers of greats like Wilt Chamberlain, Julius Erving, Bobby Jones, and Charles Barkley.

"Over here," Jayden said, as he guided me to our seats. I followed behind him and we arrived at our row. I was so impressed, but did my best to contain my sheer excitement. I liked the way Jayden moved around, but I didn't want to go giving him the wrong idea.

Once we found our seats, which were a bit tight due to the armrests, I realized there was plenty of legroom, so I was good. The cup holders were mounted on the back of the seat in front of us, and I quickly put them to use. Jayden had insisted we get beers before we found our seats.

Settled in, I glanced around as a new Jay-Z song blared through the speakers. It was still early, but they were trying to keep the mood upbeat. As the beginning of the game got closer, the lights went out and a long 76ers pump-up video was shown to get the crowd rowdy.

It worked too.

Later, after the names of the Houston Rockets' starting lineup were unceremoniously read, the Sixers' lineup got the full works. First, there was thick, white smoke. Then, each player came out of the tunnel along with a light show and fire. A ball of flames shot out from a big torch stand behind the left baseline, and that spark literally helped fuel the crowd's enthusiasm as their home-team starters ran onto the court. The roaring sound was so loud, I could've sworn the seats vibrated. After a woman stepped up to sing the "Star-Spangled Banner," the game finally started.

I was pumped and excited.

"You good?" Jayden yelled.

"Huh?"

"You good?" he repeated.

"Oh. Yeah!" I nodded quickly. "Yeah, all good over here."

Throughout the game, the entertainment really never stopped. I especially enjoyed the intimacy of the small venue combined with the electric feeling and noise level. I felt so connected to the game. A huge scoreboard with two video boards on each side and four smaller corner screens hovered over the center court.

"Where. The. Hell. Did. You. Get. These. Seats?" I yelled for the third time in Jayden's direction.

There was no other way he could make out my words. As if the loud cheering noise wasn't enough, the squeaky screeching sounds from the players' sneakers when they made a jump shot or ran along the court was even louder.

But it was all good. I was on fire. My adrenaline was pumping as we took in the sights of the players in what had to be the best seats I'd ever been in.

Jayden didn't respond; he simply raised his beer and smiled at me. He barely pulled his eyes away from the action on the court.

And who could blame him? We weren't courtside, but damn near close. The beer I'd been sipping on was just the right temperature, and I was having a blast.

The arena was so loud, but the energy was electric. We were a few seats in front of a man who held a massive megaphone. He was shirtless and had the message *"Houston You Have A Problem"* painted on his big hairy belly. It was wild!

Another man right next to him held a colorful poster that read *"We fear no beard,"* a reference to Houston's guard James Harden.

During one of the intermissions, the "Gangnam Style" Fan Cam had to be my favorite. There was nothing funnier than seeing Sixers' fans—especially the older ones—getting on camera while they did that stupid horse dance in front of nearly twenty-thousand people.

Toward the end, the Sixers were down like twenty-five points, so Jayden got up and motioned for me to do the same.

"Let's beat the crowd!" he yelled, close to my ear.

I nodded. "Okay. This was great."

He held my elbow and allowed me to walk in front of him. All in all, we had a great time. Since I wasn't a huge basketball fan, and didn't have a dog in the fight, I felt good regardless of the score.

Outside of the arena, Jayden stepped close to me. "Thank you for coming to the game with me tonight. I hope you enjoyed yourself."

I was really stunned. He had just shown me a spectacular night and he stood in front of me behaving as if I had done him a favor. I played it cool, but was still on a high on the inside.

"Oh, I'm glad I came."

"Yeah, me too," he added.

The cab ride home was quiet. I gazed out of the window as Jayden played on his phone. I suspected that he was texting his wife and probably lying about the coworker he'd gone to the game with. But that wasn't my concern. I wasn't interested in him in any way, whatsoever.

I appreciated his company. I'd been so busy with work lately, I'd almost forgotten how to have a good time.

"What are you about to do?" he asked.

My head whipped in his direction. I could hardly believe he was talking to me.

Frowning, I looked at him and said, "I'm going to bed; aren't you tired?"

"Shiiit! Tired? I'm just getting started."

"Oh, okay then. Well, go 'head, party animal," I teased.

"Are you really calling it a night?"

"Umm, yes." I crossed my legs and felt awkward when I realized his eyes had followed my every move. "Don't even think about it!" I scolded.

Jayden laughed. "You too uptight."

"Am I now?"

"Yeah; let your hair down. You're out of town. Nobody knows us here. We could do whatever the hell we want and no one would be the wiser," he said.

My right eyebrow rose. What was he getting at? Did this old school playa think he was running game? I eased back into the seat and figured I'd have some fun with his butt.

"And how do you suggest I let my hair down?"

He eyed me closely, like he was unsure of whether or not he should share his secret. Once I noticed the mischief in his eyes, I quickly spoke up and laid some ground rules.

"Whatever you're thinking is probably not gonna happen," I warned.

Jayden started laughing.

"I'm serious. I don't want any drama, and I don't want any problems."

"It ain't nothing like that; it's just a friend of mine just told me about this little private party that's going on. We don't have to go as a couple or anything like that, but you would need me in order to get in," he said.

"Little party? What kind of party?"

Jayden mischievously laughed again. "I can't tell you unless you agree to go."

CHAPTER TWENTY-NINE

Ava

As we sat in traffic, I tried to think about anything but the fight I was having with my husband. The trip to the outlets could've been worse. I didn't beat myself up over it too much. I knew better than to go there with Sylvia in the first place. But my mind wasn't really on Sylvia and her antics. It was really on if I should tell her about what was going on with Isaac.

Hours earlier, Sylvia had somewhat decided for me.

"Oh, let's go see if I can find anything for him in Calvin Klein," she'd said.

Forget about the fact that I was looking at some purses inside the Coach store.

"You go on; I wanna see how much this is gonna be after the discount." I held up the purse I was considering.

Sylvia walked closer and inspected the bag I held in my hands. She twisted her face as she tugged and pulled on parts of the bag. "Don't you have one that looks kind of like this already?" she asked.

"I don't think so."

She pulled the bag up to her shoulder and walked to a nearby mirror. I watched as Sylvia posed, turned, and looked at the bag and the way it hung off her shoulder.

"I don't like it," she said. Sylvia walked back over, and gave me the bag. "Besides, I really think you have one that looks a lot like this already."

"Maybe you're right." I put the bag back on the shelf and headed toward the door. "What are you thinking about getting for Jayden?" I asked.

"Well, you already know I'm gonna get him some running shorts and shoes, but I was thinking I'd find something else in Calvin Klein." Sylvia pulled the door open and held it for me. "You could probably find something for Isaac too."

"Humph, I'm not trying to buy shit for him." I snickered.

Sylvia stopped in her tracks. She turned to me and gave me a look that said I had spilled too much.

"Trouble in paradise?" she asked, with an eyebrow elevated.

We turned to the left and walked in the direction of the store she wanted to go into.

"Nah, I wouldn't call it paradise at all. I don't know what's wrong with that man. Lately, he's been acting a plum fool. I just walked out on his behind earlier. I'm sick of it."

"Girl. Does man trouble ever end? I mean, seriously. They are like kids most times. Well, you already know how Isaac gets, so I'm sure it's nothing serious. Sometimes, these men are worse than women on the rag."

I laughed at that, as we walked into the store. Despite the fact that I didn't want to, I found several items for Isaac, including a nice suit, a great tie, and a pair of leather loafers. I still bought them, but I told myself I'd hold them 'til Christmas if I had to. There was no way I was about to reward his recent, salty behavior.

After Sylvia paid for the outfits she'd found for Jayden, we went to the Nike store, then decided we'd had enough. I didn't want to say anything, but she'd spent an entire four hours at the outlets and although she complained, it was far more manageable that I expected.

"Hey, how's your misfit of a friend doing? You haven't talked much about her lately," Sylvia said as we got into the car.

"Who? Bailey? She's good."

"She hasn't found another blood sucker, has she?"

"Nah. She's traveling right now, but we met before she left and I'm glad to say I think she's finally starting to come around."

"You sound just like some ol' mother hen; you know that?" Sylvia said, and chuckled a bit.

Traffic was horrible and I suddenly regretted the amount of time we'd spent at the outlets. It felt like everyone decided to leave at the same time.

"You think that's how I come off?" I asked Sylvia after a few moments.

She turned back to look at me.

"What are you talking about?"

"A mother hen. You just told me I behaved like an old hen," I reminded her.

Sylvia tilted her head, as if she had to think about the answer. After a few seconds, she said, "Not really. I think there are times when you do, but overall, I wouldn't say so. I do think when it comes to Bailey, you do take on that role, but not enough where I'd give you that label on a regular basis."

I plugged in my iPod and we listened to some of our favorite music.

Suddenly, Sylvia reached over and lowered the volume.

"You planning to go back home?"

"I wasn't thinking about it, why?"

"We could go grab dinner and some drinks. You know I'm just

going home to an empty house, so I'm in no rush. But if you need to get back to Isaac and fix him some dinner, it's no biggie," she said.

I pursed my lips. "You know what? Let his behind starve. Where we going?"

"Mexican. I think I want a margarita."

"Humph. Well, I think I could use two, and a shot of Patrón too," I added.

"Well, all righty then!" Sylvia teased.

She turned the music back up and started gazing out the window. It seemed as if we'd both had tons on our minds, but for once, I didn't really feel like putting Sylvia all up in my business.

The truth was, I wasn't quite sure what was going on with Isaac myself. The last thing I wanted was for her to start carrying on about me the way we had been going on about Bailey and all of her poor choices.

Lately, I'd been thinking about what would happen if my husband lost his job. I knew for sure he would never admit it, but I really started to believe that was what he had been struggling with. If he found out they planned to let him go, he was probably beating himself up trying to figure out the best way to tell me.

"Oh, you said Bailey went out of town, where'd she go?" Sylvia asked.

I turned and looked at her.

"What'd you say?"

"Bailey. I asked you where she went. You said she went out of town on business," Sylvia repeated.

CHAPTER THIRTY

Jayden

M y return flight arrived fifteen minutes early. As I exited the aircraft and made my way toward baggage claim, I pulled out my phone and texted Sylvia to let her know that I had landed. She texted back and said that she was just pulling up, and should be there when I exited. I made it to the luggage carousel and waited for that annoying buzz and the rotating yellow light to begin spinning. Once it did, I positioned myself at the mouth of the conveyor belt so that I could grab my luggage as soon as it was spit out.

Shortly thereafter, I stood outside of the baggage claim area and looked for Sylvia. When I spotted the car, I walked over. She popped the trunk, got out, walked around to the passenger side, and got in. I tossed my suitcase in the trunk and then got behind the wheel of the vehicle.

"How was your trip?" she asked as she clicked herself into her seat belt.

"It was good, but I missed you." I leaned in and gave her a kiss. Not just a quick peck, but a passionate one that she wasn't expecting. When I pulled back from her, her eyes blinked like hazard lights.

"Whoa. Where did that come from?" she asked.

"I told you. I've missed you," I said as I put the car in gear and pulled off.

"I've missed you too." She repositioned herself in her seat. I got on the highway and headed home. Sylvia had on a summer dress. I glanced over at her thighs, placed my large hand on them, and gave her a few tender squeezes before moving my hand up upward. She put both of her hands on mine and stopped me.

"You need to pay attention before you cause an accident." Sylvia moved my hand away.

"I was only trying to get you ready."

"Ready for what?" Sylvia wanted to play dumb. I took her hand and placed it on my manhood which was firm and ready.

"This. You need to drain it," I said unashamedly.

"Jayden, I told my mother I'd drop by to see her as soon as I dropped you off at home."

"Mama has to wait. You've got business to handle when we walk in the door."

"I can take care of you when I come back," she promised as if I had just given her the option.

"I don't want to wait until you come back." I placed my hand back on her thigh. "We can go in the house, handle what needs to be done, and then you can go."

"Jayden, you don't do quickies, honey. You never have. Every time we do it, it feels like I'm in a marathon with you," she said. I wasn't sure if I had just heard a complaint or a compliment.

"What's that supposed to mean?" I asked.

"It just means that if I go in the house and screw you, I will not make it to my mother's house."

"And the problem with that would be?" I waited for an answer. She gave me an unyielding stare. All I wanted in that moment was for her to put me before her mother.

"Fuck it," I snapped bitterly and pressed the accelerator.

"I promise, as soon as I get back, I'm going to take care of you.

There is no need for you to get moody about this." She tried to win me over.

"I'm cool." I turned up the radio. "Gangnam Style" played, and I immediately thought about how much fun I'd had with Bailey and began singing.

"Eh, sexy lady!" I bellowed out as I tapped the steering wheel with my thumb.

"Wait, hold the hell up. What in the world do you know about this song?" Sylvia looked at me as if my head was on backward.

"Broken condom style. Eh, sexy lady!" I continued to move to the groove.

"What the hell is 'broken condom style'?" Sylvia asked.

"He's singing all of the words, except the chorus, in Korean. I don't know what the hell he's saying, so I made up some words that made sense to me. Eh, sexy lady!"

"Okay, you are just too damn much for me to handle." Sylvia continued to glare at me as if I had switched from noon to midnight in an instant.

"Eh, sexy lady?" I sang to Sylvia, but I thought about Bailey.

"What in the hell did you do while you were out there?" Sylvia turned off the music.

"Hey, turn that back on," I complained.

"No. Answer my damn question!" Sylvia had caught an attitude.

"Want me to fix that uptight attitude for you?" I smiled.

"Oh, hell no. I'm gonna do what I need to do with my mama and then when I come back, I'll have something for yo' ass," Sylvia promised. Thirty minutes later, I pulled up in front of the house, got my suitcase out of the trunk, and said goodbye.

Sylvia looked at me for a long time, and wondered who or what I had transformed into. She finally pulled off and I went inside.

Once I got settled in, I decided to give Isaac a buzz to find out

how he was doing and also to tell him about the wild time that I'd
had in Philadelphia.

"Yo," I said when I heard him pick up the phone on the other end.

"Yo." He returned the greeting.

"What's going on?"

"The usual bullshit."

"Where are you? What's all of that noise I hear?" I asked.

"I'm driving and have the window down."

"Where are you headed?"

"Home right now, but I'm not looking forward to going inside," Isaac admitted.

"Do you want to meet up at a bar for some drinks?"

"Sounds like a good idea to me. I could use a cold one."

We made plans to meet up at a sports bar in about an hour. I
placed my luggage in the laundry room so that I could wash my
clothes once I returned. I took a quick shower and then headed
out the door.

An hour later, I sat at a bar and waited on Isaac while I chewed
salty peanuts and drank a beer. A basketball game was on the television, but my favorite team wasn't playing. As I enjoyed my cold
one, I paid attention to a few attractive women. One in particular
had a shapely figure and a nice bottom. She was young, late twenties, and looked to me be a mixture of African American and
Asian. She was rather exotic-looking and that primal part of me
wanted to pull off my wedding band, shove it in my pocket, and
strike up a conversation with her and the girlfriend that she was
hanging out with. Just as I was about to do that, Isaac appeared.

"Oh, there you are," he said and approached me. I smiled at him
and tilted my head in the direction of the two ladies.

"If we play our cards right, we could have some fun." My foolish
ego spoke before I had a chance to think.

"Man, calm down," Isaac said, uninterested.

I chuckled. "Damn, man, there is nothing wrong with talking to someone. Talking to people can lead to some very interesting activities." Isaac took a seat and then looked over his shoulder at the young ladies.

"They're nice-looking," he admitted.

"You're damn right they are." I paused briefly and placed my hand on his shoulder. "Dude, I have got to tell you what went down while I was out of town."

"Hang on a minute," Isaac said. He got the attention of the bartender and ordered a whiskey sour. Once Isaac had his drink, he gulped it down like water running down a drain and ordered another one. I got concerned about the way he guzzled down his alcohol, but decided not to address it.

"All right, lay it on me. What happened?" he asked.

"Okay, remember how I told you I met this woman while I was out there, right?"

"You said you met someone, but that you hadn't hooked up."

"Well, we did end up hanging out."

"Where did you guys go?" Isaac asked.

"First I took her to a 76ers game." I took a drink of my beer.

"Did you have good seats?"

"Come on, man, you know me. Of course I had good seats." I met his gaze.

"Okay, my bad." Isaac tossed up his hands. "So did you hit it after the game?" he prodded, wanting to jump ahead in the story.

"No. After the game, she was going to call it a night and head back to her room, but I told her that I still wanted to hang out. At first she didn't feel like it, but then she changed her mind."

"What made her change her mind?" Isaac asked.

"When I told her where I was heading to." I laughed.

"And where was that?"

"To a ballet performance."

Isaac looked at me as if I had just spit in his drink. "You and your weird artsy shit. Only you would go to the ballet after a basketball game. You should have taken her ass to the hotel bar and got her drunk out of her mind," Isaac said.

"It was the naked ballet." I let the cat out of the bag.

"The what?" Isaac repositioned himself to make sure he had heard me correctly.

"I took her to the naked ballet," I repeated.

"What the fuck is that?"

"I swear, you're an uncultured mofo. It's a dance performance where everyone dances naked," I explained.

"The women too?" Isaac asked for clarity.

"Absolutely," I said.

"Now that's some freaky shit. What did your date think about that?"

"She was game. She had never been to anything like it. The dancers' moves were very sensual, and since we were right up front, we got to see it all. My date got hotter than a brick oven. I could tell by the way she wiggled around in her seat. If I had to guess, I'd say it has been a long time since she's had her legs in the air."

"Well, did you seal the deal? Did you hit it?" Isaac asked.

"No. Lord knows that I wanted to. The early dawn cab ride back to the hotel was tense. She snuggled up next to me and I asked her if we could take it to the next level before my flight left."

"What did she say?"

"She said that if we had more time she'd show me a thing or two, but she wasn't about to let me hit it and then run out the door. So, she asked for my number for a rain check and I gave it to her. I told her to call me when she was ready to play."

"That's it?" Isaac asked.

"That's it. What about you? How is your little situation going?"

Isaac called the bartender over and ordered another drink. "I talked to Denise and told her that I didn't appreciate her going to the Public Assistance office on me."

"What did she say?"

"She told me to be careful of what I say to her." Isaac paused. "She's got me by the fucking balls, man."

"You need to go on and tell Ava."

Isaac's drink arrived and he took a hard swallow. "Not yet."

The way he avoided disclosing his secret was like cancer that infected his mind. As I looked at Isaac, I noticed how exhausted his eyes were. The burden of the secret he carried was clearly too much.

CHAPTER THIRTY-ONE

Bailey

I sniffled and tried to pull myself together as much as possible. I know I must've sounded like a complete wreck, but I didn't know what else to do. The police wanted me to come down to the station to look at a lineup, or answer some questions. I just didn't have the strength to go alone.

"Maybe I should call Ava," I muttered, as I looked through my phone. I shook my head. "Nah, I'm not calling her. Lord knows it took long enough for her to forget about my stupid mistake of trusting Michael in the first doggone place. Since we were well past that, the last thing I wanted to do was give her a reason to think about it again."

Just as I was about to turn off the phone and contemplate my options, his number all but popped up at me.

"Damn. Why didn't I think about that before? Would it be so wrong for me to call him?" I looked at the screen and went over in my mind all of the reasons why calling him would be my best option.

"To hell with it," I said, as I pressed the button to dial his number.

My heart rang out louder in my ear than the ringing on the other end. With each ring, my courage slipped a little more. What if he didn't even remember me? I knew that would be near impossible, but still, married men who were out on a pass tended to forget what they did while they were away from home.

After I released a deep breath, I decided not to leave a voicemail message. The last thing I wanted was for his wife to intercept it. I'd been down that road before and wasn't trying to go back.

I got up and walked over to the closet. If I had to face that bastard again, I wanted to make sure I looked my absolute best. There was no way I could forget how Michael cleaned me out and vanished, but I had done my best over the last few months to keep the past behind me. Now, the thought of facing him, after all he had done, made me a bit nervous. When my cell phone rang, I nearly jumped over the bed to grab it before voicemail could.

"Hello?" My heart raced. Deep down, I was praying it would be Jayden calling back. Unfortunately for me, it was the detective.

"Hi, Ms. Jones, we need to know whether you are available to come help us out with a lineup."

"Umm, I suppose so," I finally said flatly.

"Okay, well, if you can meet me down at 1401 Broadway, we won't take up much of your time. Be sure to ask for Captain Willis."

The officer was pleasant enough. I appreciated the fact that they really were trying to help locate Michael's trifling behind, but there was still that part of me that hoped he'd never be found. Well, I guess it's time for me to put my big girl panties on. I eased up from the bed and went to pull the two outfits I'd selected for the grim occasion.

It had been a week since the trip to Philly and I hadn't heard from Jayden. Not that I expected to hear from him. It wasn't like we were bosom buddies now, but I would've expected at least a quick call to hear he had made it okay. If I was talking to Ava about my personal life, I'd be able to brag about the fact that I had met this handsome man who'd had it all together, hung out with him for days, and didn't screw him. That was a new record for me, but I knew there was no way I could share it with anyone.

I slipped into the black tuxedo pants and found a blue silk shirt. I grabbed a gold glitter belt and a pair of pointy-toe pumps. I was ready to go. As I looked over my reflection in the mirror, the phone rang again. I rolled my eyes. I told the officer I was coming; what more did he want? I was more than a little irritated as I snatched the phone, swiped my finger across the screen, and answered.

"Hello?"

"Oh, hey, Ms. Jones. I forgot to tell you. Park across the street in the lot and bring your ticket for validation," the officer said.

"Okay. Thanks. And I will see you soon."

When I started to think about the reason I was headed down to the police station, a sense of sadness and fear settled back in again. What would happen if I did finger Michael? I wonder whether pointing him out would be like it was on those police dramas on TV. Would I be in a room, behind a two-way mirror?

What if he got out and came over to deal with me for snitching? There was no way in hell I could do this alone.

I grabbed my cell phone. I'd have to deal with Ava's smart comments after all. When I swiped my finger across the screen, a caller was there.

"Hello?"

"Hey, Bailey."

"Yeah?"

"It's me, Jayden. I saw a missed call from you," he said.

"Oh. Did you call me back?"

The awkward pause didn't last long, but his tone of voice told me he was confused.

"Yeah. I did. When I realized there was a missed call, I picked up my phone and dialed you back."

I told myself to forget the fact that he sounded like he was explaining a simple equation to a toddler. I needed his help.

"I was just asking. I was about to use the phone and I was a little surprised to hear you on the other end," I said. I sighed really hard.

"Hey, what's up? You don't sound so good. Is everything okay?"

"You know what, I shouldn't even bother you with this," I said.

"Oh, try me. I'm sure it's no bother at all. What's up?"

"Well, a few months ago, before I met you, someone I knew and trusted ripped me off. The police think they've found him, and they want me to come down to the station to answer some questions or pick him out of a lineup. Honestly, I'm not sure what they want me to do. All I know is they want me to come down there, and I really don't feel up to going alone."

"So, you were hoping I'd agree to go with you?"

"Well, yeah, sort of," I said.

"Of course I'll come with you. You wanna meet there or you want me to come by your place?"

My heart started to race. I was as excited as a kid on Christmas Eve.

"You will? I mean, you'd do that for me?"

"Sure. We're friends, aren't we?"

"Yeah. But what about your wife?" I asked.

"Uh, what about her? You don't plan to give me a blow job or anything like that, do you?"

He made me laugh. "No, silly."

"Oh, okay then. My wife shouldn't have a problem with it then. I mean, if I get over there and you decide you want to sit on my face or something like that, then, she might have a problem. But me escorting a scared friend to the police department shouldn't be an issue."

I felt 100 percent better after talking with him. Jayden agreed to meet at my place and offered to drive me to the station. He was a good guy, and I was so glad we had met and nothing had happened between us. Maybe that was exactly what I needed, a good guy who could accept me as just a friend.

Once I hung up with Jayden, I rushed to my closet and swapped out my dark, dreary outfit for a flirty, ruffled wrap dress that was a loud, burnt-orange color. Knowing I wouldn't have to go through this alone had already lifted my spirits.

CHAPTER THIRTY-TWO

Ava

I wondered what kind of day this would be as I walked down the carpeted stairs. I was more than tired of moving around my house with a stranger. The more I thought about it, my husband wasn't the only stranger in my life.

Both of my girls had gone and lost their minds and I didn't know who was the craziest. I had given Isaac the silent treatment for three days before I decided to soften and gave in. The truth was, I was simply tired of the drama. That was not our life. I left the drama to Bailey and I didn't want to change that. Thinking about my husband and his strange behavior only made me want to slap the taste out of his mouth. But then I realized he was just a man.

That meant he didn't really know how to express himself and whatever he might have been going through. It was just as I had suspected all along. The man was tripping and going crazy over some stuff at work.

If I didn't know Isaac like the back of my hand, I didn't know myself. I walked into the kitchen, and spied him as he sat there looking like a statue. He stared off into space, as if he was heavily sedated. At first, I considered letting him have his peace and behaving as if I never even saw him. But when I realized that he really was in a zone, it made me feel kind of weird about how I had been treating my husband since he started behaving strangely.

"Baby," I said softly. I figured if my voice was sweet and soft, he'd be more receptive.

He didn't answer.

Isaac gave me a dismissive shrug, but never uttered a word.

It wasn't easy, but I didn't get mad. I fixed the drink I knew I'd need, and walked over to the table where he sat.

"Babe," I said, as I eased onto the chair. "What's been going on with you?"

His wide eyes scared me. Had my husband turned to drugs? He had been acting very strange. When he turned to look at me, I didn't know what to expect. I was relieved to see that his pupils weren't dilated, but his eyes looked lost. That's when it hit my heart. I hadn't been the kind of wife I needed to be. My man was clearly in turmoil, and I was busy being pissed that he had been acting weird.

I got up from my seat and walked over to put my arms around him. When Isaac leaned into my torso, I felt the connection we'd had for many years.

"It's okay, babe; you can tell me what's going on. I know things at work may not be going the way you wanted or the way you planned, but we can tackle this together."

When I felt him lean into me, I wondered how long he had been carrying whatever was bothering him. He was like most men who felt they couldn't open up to their woman.

"Are you scared you're gonna lose your job or something?" I asked. He didn't answer that question, but when he looked up at me, the sadness in his eyes told me I had hit the nail on the head.

My husband had always been a pillar of strength the entire time we'd been together. To see him reduced to a state of weakness made me feel uncomfortable, but I couldn't let him see me fall apart.

"We can downsize, you know," I said. I took his face into my hands and looked him in the eyes. "We have lived below our means for many, many years. Quit, baby; we will be okay. I don't like the way you've been walking around here like a zombie. If they don't appreciate you, if they don't know the gem they have in you, then leave. You know I will stand by your side, no matter what. You remember when we were first married and we ate beans for a whole month so we could save up for our first car?"

My husband closed his eyes and shook his head.

"Baby, I've been riding with you from day one. Ain't a damn thing changed. Whatever you want to do, let's do it!"

He still didn't say anything, but I could feel his pain. Isaac had given everything to his job. He worked seventy to eighty hour weeks and this is how they treated him? Now I was pissed.

"Listen to me," I said firmly. "We will survive if you take some time off. Hell, you can go out on stress leave, or better yet, you can just quit. I don't care what you do, I just want my husband back. Lately, I've been dealing with just a shell of you and I'm ready for this to be over." You know what? Let's take a vacation! We can go on a cruise, or we can go to Jamaica!"

The faraway look in his eyes seemed to diminish a bit and I felt encouraged. Maybe he just needed to hear me say that I really was in his corner.

Isaac adjusted himself so that he could look at my face.

I thought he wanted to hear more about us taking a trip together.

"We can invite Sylvia and Jayden," I said. "It can be a couple's thing, or if you want, we can go alone. The point is, I think we are both long overdue for a nice, romantic vacation."

Unable to read his expression, I kept talking. "You know, the more I think about it, maybe we should make it a romantic getaway for two. We don't need anyone weighing us down. I think we need some alone time just to reconnect."

"Have a seat, Ava," he said.

The sound of his voice moved me. I felt drunk with excitement. Obviously something I had said had finally resonated with him. I reached back for the chair and guided myself into my seat. I didn't want to take my eyes off of him for fear he might fall back into that state he'd been in for a while lately.

"Okay, baby, what's going on?" I asked.

Isaac cleared his throat. He blinked a few times and looked like he needed to search for the proper words.

I felt my heart threaten to stop. *What if he was about to tell me that he had already quit?* In my mind, I decided to try and practice being calm.

"Listen." He cleared his throat again. "I need to talk to you about something." He took my hands into his and began to rub them.

I was happy. Finally, he was about to let me in. I smiled.

"Okay, babe, what's going on?" I asked again.

Isaac closed his eyes and slowly shook his head. That's when my eyebrows knitted into one. *Wait, was this about the trouble at work or not?* I frowned and tilted my head slightly to the side.

"Babe? What's going on?"

"Ava, there's something I need to tell you and I don't know how to say it."

My heart stopped dead in my chest.

CHAPTER THIRTY-THREE

Jayden

I was surprised that Bailey had called me. I thought I would not hear from her again. As I sat at my desk, I thought about what we could do after she completed her business at the police station. Then it hit me. I could take her out for drinks, which would help her to unwind, and I could see how things progressed from there.

I picked up the phone on my desk and called Sylvia. The phone rang several times before she picked up.

"Hey, baby," she answered. I heard the smile in her voice.

"Hey, babes. If you have any plans for us this evening, I was calling to let you know that I would be home late."

"That's fine. I was actually going to call you to let you know that I was going to stop by my mother's house on my way home. You should pick yourself up something to eat."

"I will," I said and momentarily wondered why I did not feel an ounce of guilt about how I intended to spend my evening. It was a red flag that something was seriously wrong, but I pushed those thoughts aside and buried them.

"By the way, my car has been acting funny lately. I'm gonna need for you to take it for a drive and determine if it needs to go into the shop."

"What's it doing?" I asked, welcoming a different subject to focus on.

"It makes a scrubbing sound sometimes when I press down on the brakes," Sylvia said.

"Then it's probably time to have them replaced. I'll take it out this weekend."

"Oh, baby. I have to call you later. Ava is trying to call me."

"Okay. I'll talk to you later. No need to wait up for me," I said and hung up. I sat and stared at the phone. I thought Sylvia would call me right back and ask for more details, but she didn't. I then gathered up my belongings and headed out to meet Bailey.

An hour later, I sat and waited patiently with her on a hard, wooden bench inside the police station. She had already checked in with the desk sergeant who asked her to have a seat until she was called.

"Thank you for coming down here with me on such short notice. I know that you must have better things you could be doing with your time." Bailey reached over and touched my hand.

"It's really not a problem. I'm glad I could be of support. Although I am curious as to why you wanted me to come and not a girl-friend," I said.

She huffed. "Because I would have had to listen to their dispar-aging remarks and I just don't need to hear those types of negative comments."

"I see." I repositioned myself on the bench in such a way that we appeared more like a couple than casual acquaintances. "After we leave here, would you like to go out for a cocktail?"

"I would absolutely love to," she agreed. I crossed one leg over the other and Bailey placed the palm of her hand on my knee. I could tell that she did it out of nervousness, but in my mind, I made the touch out to be a sexual one.

"Ma'am, you're here to view a lineup, correct?" asked a uniformed officer.

"Yes," Bailey answered nervously.

"Please come with me."

Bailey turned to me. "I'm going to leave my purse here."

I nodded my head, indicating that it would be safe with me. I watched Bailey as she trailed behind the officer who led her through a door on the opposite side of the room.

A short time later, she returned. She folded some paperwork in half so that it could fit comfortably in her purse.

"How did it go?" I asked.

"I could really use that drink." Bailey ignored my question.

"Come on; I know a place that is not too far from here."

It wasn't long before Bailey and I were positioned at the bar. She ordered wine, and I ordered a vodka and cranberry juice.

"So now will you tell me how it went?" I leaned in close to her.

"Michael, the guy who ripped me off, he wasn't in that lineup. But all of this, it's just too much." Bailey took a deep gulp of her wine.

I was a pretty good judge of a person's behavior and body language, and I could tell that Bailey was looking to get tipsy as quickly as possible so that she didn't have to focus on what she had just gone through.

"Well, one good thing is, at least you know they're looking for the loser." I offered her as much comfort as I could.

"Yes, I guess so. They think he's part of an elaborate network that the police infiltrated." Bailey finished her drink and ordered another round.

"Those types of people should be locked up," I said.

"You got that right."

"So what happens next?"

"They'll keep me posted. I'll be contacted again when they think they've found him. It's an undercover officer working with the group, so they can't be sure who is who." Bailey repositioned herself and looked at me. The wine had begun to have the effect that she was after.

"So what did you think about our time in Philly?" I asked.

Bailey smiled. "I will admit that I have never in my life attended a naked ballet." She smirked.

"Did you like it?"

Bailey craned her neck, met my gaze, and held onto it. Her gaze was so intense, I swear that I heard her innermost thoughts. "The ballet was hot and it had me feeling some kinda way. So let's just say that if I had decided to be a bad girl, you would have had the time of your life."

"Oooh, now we're getting somewhere," I said. I ordered myself another drink.

"Slow down. I said if, not when." Bailey wanted to be very clear.

"Okay, I can respect that. So if you had been a bad girl, tell me something I could have looked forward to."

"For starters, I would have come back to your room and given you the best blow job of your life."

I almost dropped my drink when she said that. "Damn." I thought about what that would feel like.

Bailey chuckled. "You're not ready for an experience with me. I'll have you confused."

"Oh, I don't think that's possible," I said and then decided to be bold. I placed my hand on her thigh and squeezed it a few times.

"Be careful; you're playing with fire," Bailey warned me.

I leaned in, placed my cheek next to hers, and spoke in her ear. "Well, it's a good thing I have a giant hose that puts out fires."

"I'll give you that. I noticed the bulge in your slacks. You might be carrying something I could really use after the experience I had in the station today." Bailey sloshed down the remaining wine in her glass and ordered another round.

"Well, we should go someplace and find out if what I have is what you need." I leaned in again and gave her a kiss on the cheek. She placed her hand on my chest and gently pushed me away.

"You're playing a dangerous game, Jayden."

"We both are," I said. She looked at me again and sipped more of her wine. Her eyes had turned glassy. She smiled and laughed more than she needed to.

"What the hell. I don't feel like denying myself tonight." Bailey had given in to the moment.

"That's what I'm talking about. Just go with the flow. I'm into you and you're into me. We're two adults who can do whatever we want to." I wanted to seal the deal. I wanted to have my fun with her and that's all I cared about at that moment.

"Hotel room?" She looked at me and raised an eyebrow.

"Works for me," I said as I listened to the egoistical voice in my head shout out as if my favorite team had just scored the game-winning touchdown.

"I'm gonna run to the ladies' room. When I come back, well, you know." She winked at me before she walked away, rocking her hips as she slinked through the crowd. I licked my lips and took another sip of my drink. I felt my phone vibrating on my hip. I removed it from its holster and answered it.

"Yo," I spoke into the phone.

"Jayden, it's me, man." I heard Isaac's voice.

"Dude, you ain't gonna believe this, but—"

Isaac interrupted me before I could finish. "Jayden, I need your help."

"What?" I laughed. I thought he was joking.

"I need your help. I need to borrow some money. I'll get it back to you as soon as I can though."

"Money?"

"Ava knows, man. I told her and she put me out. I need to get a hotel room for a few days and I'm a little strapped for cash right now because of my situation." Isaac's call threatened to ruin my fun.

"You know your timing is real fucked up, right?" My voice was filled with condemnation.

"I'm in a bad way, Jayden. I'm asking you as my friend. Can you help or let me crash at your place for a minute? I'll stay in the attic above your garage if I have to. I really don't want to go to my parents' house."

"No. I'll loan you some money. If Ava's pissed at you, then that means Sylvia knows about it as well." I paused for a moment when I saw Bailey heading back toward me. She was still rocking her hips and judging by the way she approached me without taking her eyes off of me, I knew that she was fully committed to having her way with me.

"Listen, Isaac, you're my boy, right?"

"Of course I am," he said.

"Are you in your car?"

"Yeah."

"I'm going to need you to go someplace and sit tight until I call you back. There is something that I've just got to take care of first," I said, and hung up the phone.

CHAPTER THIRTY-FOUR

Bailey

I wanted the liquor to burn away my misery. It had been months since I'd been with a man, and after what had happened with Michael, or whatever the hell his name was, I wanted every single memory scorched away with something equivalent to the 190-proof grain alcohol, Everclear.

Since I didn't want my new friend, Jayden, to think I was some irresponsible drunk, I played it safe with wine. Inside the bathroom, as I looked at my reflection in the mirror, his words replayed in my head.

It's a good thing I have a giant hose that puts out fires...

"I wanna see what he's working with. Hell, I just wanna get my back pushed out tonight," I muttered to my reflection.

I toyed with the pros and cons of screwing Jayden, and even the cons started to feel like pros when I felt my wet panties.

He was married, so I could have a little fun and send him back home to his wife. Let him be her problem. Since he had everything in the world to lose, I wouldn't have to worry about any issues.

"Just this one time," I said to the mirror.

After washing my hands, I pressed powder over my shining nose, added more lip gloss, and pursed my lips. Once my face was back together, I turned to look at my ass in the mirror.

"Okay, all good. Now let's go have some fun!"

When I strutted back to the bar and saw Jayden having an animated phone conversation, I beckoned the bartender close.

"Another glass of wine?" he asked.

"Nah, enough of that. I'd like Crown Royal on ice."

His eyes widened and he smiled.

"All righty then," he said and winked.

When I saw him pull out a fancy cocktail glass, I gestured for him to stop.

"Had a change of heart?"

"Oh, no, just want you to change the glass. You don't have to dress it up for me."

"Okay," he said, and winked again before he turned away to fix my drink.

Jayden returned and I smiled.

"We still on?"

"Yeah, we're good," I said, and looked toward the bartender who slid a new drink in front of me.

"Whoa! What'd I miss?" Jayden asked. He looked at me, the drink, and back at the bartender.

"Nothing," I said. I lifted the glass from the bar, "Dark liquor makes me hot and horny as hell, and I wanted to make sure I gave you my all tonight."

"So you're on fire then?" he said with a friendly chuckle.

"Oh, daddy, I will be after about one more of these." I gulped the drink down.

When I finished, the look on Jayden's face was one of utter surprise.

"Oh, you're serious?"

He waved the bartender over and said, "Give us another round for the road." Once the bartender nodded, he turned his attention back to me. "I don't know if you should be driving after all that."

"Oh, I'm good." When I hiccupped loudly, I stopped speaking. I brought a hand up to my lips and smiled. "I'm sorry."

"No worries. Listen, let's wrap this up and go."

The bartender brought his vodka and my Crown. This time, I didn't swallow it down like I did the first drink. When we were done, Jayden looked at me with curious eyes.

"You gonna be okay?" Jayden asked like he was unsure.

"Oh. I'm good. Let's go."

He paid the bill and gestured for me to go ahead of him. I loved when a man touched me in the small of my back like he did as I passed him.

"So here's what we're gonna do. We'll leave your car here and take mine. Then when we're done, you can come back for yours."

I shook my head and put my hands on my hips. The liquor was doing its job, but I felt good.

"I told you. I'm good," I protested.

"Yeah. And I believe you, but I just wanna play it safe. I don't want you behind the wheel after all you've been drinking."

When I turned and stumbled, I was glad he stood there to talk to me. He had to catch me.

"Oh gosh, I'm sorry."

"Listen, we're good. Let's go."

As I sat in the passenger seat of his car, I felt my head swim a little. My stomach also started to feel a little woozy.

As he drove, Jayden kept stealing glances in my direction. "You okay over there?"

"I'm good. I'm on fire, daddy."

I frowned a little when he laughed.

"For real. I'm good. I'm hot and ready. I'm ready for that big ol' hose you was talking 'bout," I slurred a bit.

"Okay, okay. Well, hang on, we're almost there."

Nearly thirty minutes later, we were walking into the hotel room and I was ready to pounce. Suddenly, Jayden looked at me, and his expression made me nervous.

"Dude! Seriously, I told you. I'm good." I pulled the shoulder of my dress down and wiggled out of it. As I stood there in my bra, panties, and high heels, I felt like I had his attention.

"Damn! Your body is tight," Jayden said.

I pulled his hand up to my breast and said, "Enough talking, let's see that hose you were bragging about."

Before he could respond or react, I moved in closer and reached down to stroke his crotch. When he tried to kiss me, I turned my head and he started sucking on my neck.

I clung to him tightly as he sucked at my neck harder and more aggressively. A few buttons here, a zipper there, and off came his shirt and pants.

He ran his finger along the lace trim of my panties like it was a delicate commodity.

"Rip them off," I whispered. "Rip them off and fuck me."

Jayden did exactly what I told him to do. I could tell by the way he tugged at my panties that it turned him on. He seemed excited and hungry with passion.

"Condom. You can't go raw with me."

Jayden pulled back and looked at me with confusion on his face. "I don't have—"

"It's okay. I'm always prepared." I grabbed the condom and ripped it open. Then I put it in my mouth.

Jayden's eyes grew wide. I shoved him back onto the sofa, then dropped to my knees between his legs. As he watched, I lowered my head into his lap and sucked down onto his large, stiff dick.

He released a moan, as I nearly gagged.

"Damn, girl," he said as I rose.

I turned my back to him and threw one leg over his. Then I eased down onto his stiff erection. My eyes grew wide as I wiggled my hips and felt him swell inside of me. I inhaled a deep breath and held it until he was nestled comfortably inside my slippery, wet folds.

"Oh shit, Jayden," I cried.

He began to thrust as he cupped my breasts from behind.

"Oh, God," I cried, and bit down on my bottom lip.

I turned to face him, and Jayden dipped his head down and took one of my stiffened nipples into his mouth. He sucked it as if it was the sweetest taste to touch his lips.

When he came up for air, I closed my eyes and tried my best to live in the moment. *Who knew when I'd be able to have a man in my arms again?*

"Take it," he panted.

One minute, I was immersed in the sheer pleasure he was giving; the next, I was telling myself there was no way I could or should get used to this. He was unavailable; he was off limits and this was only temporary.

I hooked my leg around his waist, and used my nails to dig into his back. Then I remembered he was borrowed goods. I couldn't send him back with passion marks or signs that I had worked him over. I cleared my mind. I was thinking far too much and too hard.

"You like this?" he asked.

"Oh, yes! Yes, fuck me. Fuck me harder, Jayden. Fuck me!"

That's exactly what he did. I felt every single inch of him in that position. He worked his hips and seemed to go even deeper, long after I thought he had reached his limit.

"Damn! It's so… You're so fucking good," I cried.

Jayden ground himself into me, and I could have melted.

CHAPTER THIRTY-FIVE

Ava

"So he just up and left?" Sylvia asked. Her face was almost frozen into a menacing scowl. She sucked her teeth and rolled her eyes as she paced the area behind my sofa. I could've sworn she was about to wear the carpet out.

"I'm trying to tell you. Something ain't right. I don't know exactly what's going on, but I know Isaac and I know something ain't right."

Sylvia stopped her pace to look at me.

"What do you mean? Do you think he's having an affair? Girl, I'm glad you put his ass out. If it was me, I'd be in jail somewhere," Sylvia said.

"You don't understand. We don't have that kind of relationship. My husband and I have always been real, real close, so when he started acting all strange, I knew something was up, but I wasn't sure what. Then I remembered one of his coworkers who I helped out with a real delicate situation," I said.

Sylvia moved closer.

"What are you talking about? Is she screwing your man, or does she know who is?"

"Girl. I don't think it's anything like that. Seriously. I know Isaac, and I know his patterns. He ain't looking for a new woman. I really think it has something to do with work," I said.

The way Sylvia looked at me made me feel like I was a special head case. Everything about her expression said, *If you don't see the writing on the wall, the proof that your husband is cheating, then I have some swamp land I want to sell you in my backyard.*

"Who's to say he's looking? What if he already has someone? I told you to let me put the private investigator on him. We would've found all of the information we needed," she said.

Sylvia made me feel like I didn't have my shit together. I know we would spend time talking about Bailey, and all that she was doing wrong. But now she was making me feel like I didn't know right from wrong when it came to men.

"Girl, I've been married to this man long enough to know how he operates." I threw my hands up. "You know what? Let's not talk about this anymore. I'm so done I don't know what else to say about this. He's gone and until he talks to me, I don't want to see his ass!"

Sylvia looked at her phone and frowned again; then she put it back down.

I needed to change the subject. I didn't want to talk about Isaac anymore. I didn't want to think about why my husband was gone or how long he'd be gone. I only asked Sylvia over since I didn't feel like going out myself. I was in a pissy mood.

But the truth was, she made me feel even worse. I wondered why I had even called her in the first, damn place. I couldn't call Bailey. *What would I look like telling her something after I tried my best to warn her about that loser she'd moved into her place?*

"Where's Jayden?" I asked Sylvia.

I didn't really care about her husband's whereabouts. I was simply tired of her dumping on mine.

She stopped and whipped her head in my direction. "I don't know.

I mean, he went somewhere, but I haven't talked to him again."

Sylvia sounded kind of lost, but who was I to talk about any-body else's man? Mine was gone. I still couldn't wrap my mind around why.

I'd thought we were off to a good discussion about the issues going on at work. Then suddenly, he'd jumped up, screamed at me, slammed his hands onto the table and stormed out of the room.

I should've left him alone. I should've given him time to cool off, but I felt like I was close to figuring out what was going on with my man.

When he turned on me and literally morphed into the devil him-self, I told him to leave.

"You don't get to talk to me like that and share the same space I breathe," I said.

"Oh, I'll leave!"

"Then get to moving! Get out!"

"Oh, you're gonna regret this. You're gonna regret this, for real. I ain't gotta beg nobody for their love, I know somebody who will—"

When Isaac stopped cold as if he wanted to kick himself for admitting too much, I knew in my heart of hearts.

My eyes filled with tears that burned at the corners. I was at a complete loss for words.

Before I knew what was happening, my husband had his arms up in a defensive manner and I found myself on him.

"You son of a bitch! You're cheating on me?" I screamed and cried, as I tried to pummel him with my fists.

I grabbed the broom and started swinging wildly in his direction.

"Stop trippin'!" he hollered, as he jumped back, dodged, and ducked to avoid being hit. "You need to quit."

Believing my husband had screwed someone else was a blow to the gut that I wasn't expecting.

Every time I stepped out of the house, a man was looking at me like he wanted a moment of my time—the lawn men, men at the grocery store, on my way to work. It was like I was a man magnet, and no matter how hard they tried, I always said no. All of these years, I'd remained faithful to my husband. Yet, he couldn't say the same.

"What are you over there doing, daydreaming?" Sylvia asked and brought my thoughts back to the issue at hand.

I turned to look at her and asked, "When did we get old? When did we decide being at home and complaining about our men was the epitome of a great evening?"

Sylvia had a blank expression on her face. She behaved as if she wasn't sure how to answer my question.

"I feel like a bona fide old-ass lady, Sylvia. We're barely forty, but we act like we're seventy!" I sighed hard.

Sylvia plopped down on the couch across from me.

"Honey, I'm sorry you're going through this shit. But you absolutely did the right thing. I'm glad you put his worthless ass out. Maybe he'll think twice before he decides to go and screw someone else."

I heard her words, but the truth was, I didn't want to believe that my husband had done that. In my heart of hearts, I felt like that's exactly what he had done, but suddenly, I started to think about the kind of advice I might give to Bailey.

That's when it hit me. I snatched my cell phone and called Isaac.

CHAPTER THIRTY-SIX

Jayden

I could tell that Bailey had not had her legs in the air in some time. She was energetic and adventurous in bed. The journey of discovering Bailey and her magic spots excited me. It was the sensual breathing sounds she made and the way her body trembled when I found a sensitive spot. It was also the way I had made her scream into the pillow so that we wouldn't disturb our hotel neighbors.

"Damn, I am going to feel you for days!" Bailey cried out.

"Damn right you are," I spoke in her ear as I kept pumping her until I had worked up my own orgasm.

"Oh my God, I feel you; cum for me, Jayden," It was the way Bailey said those words. It was as if she lived for that explosive moment of pleasure. She pleaded with me again and again to release my essence.

"Cum for me, Jayden. I want to feel you." I closed my eyes as sweat dripped from my body and I felt myself reach the point of no return. Finally, I released. I stayed inside of her for a long moment, enjoying delightful aftershocks before I rolled onto my back. Bailey crossed her legs at her ankles. We both breathed heavily as we allowed our sweaty bodies to cool down.

"I hope you've got more left in you." Bailey was still hot and that thrilled me. She got on her knees, removed the condom I had on, and took me into the cave of her mouth. She circled her tongue around my shaft and nearly drove me up the wall. Bailey sucked and tugged on me as if I was her favorite dessert. As I looked down at her doing me, I thought, *Sylvia had never been as enthusiastic about oral sex as Bailey.*

After Bailey and I had exhausted ourselves, we took a shower together. I enjoyed washing and caressing her body and was already thinking about hooking up with her again.

"Well, we'd better hurry up. I've had my fun and now it's time to send you back home," Bailey said.

"I'm not on a clock."

"Whatever, Jayden. Just hurry up so that you can take me back to my car," she said. She stepped out of the shower.

"Hand me a towel, please." As I dried my skin, Bailey turned and stared at me for a long moment. She took all of me in, judging and making mental notes.

"It's a goddamn shame."

"What do you mean?" I asked as I placed the towel on the rack and stood naked before her.

"You've got a beautiful Johnson dangling between your thighs and your wife doesn't appreciate it. Women can be really dumb sometimes. Men are so easy to please. You guys aren't complicated like we are. If you were my man, you damn sure would not be looking outside of my bedroom for pleasure."

"So you like this?" I pointed to my Pride. Bailey smiled.

"I like it as much as you like this ass." She smacked her behind. Bailey and I exited the bathroom and began getting dressed. I glanced at my cell phone and noticed that Isaac had called numerous times and had left several voicemail and text messages. I opened up a text message.

In the emergency room, getting treatment.

"What the fuck?" I spoke louder than I had intended to.

"Don't tell me some shit, like your wife, followed you here." Bailey panicked.

"No, it's not that. My buddy is in the emergency room. We've got to hurry up so that I can get you back to your car and go see about him," I said, then dialed his number.

"Yo, man, what's up?" I asked when Isaac picked up the phone.

"I'm in the emergency room."

"What happened?"

"I needed you, man, but you played me." Isaac attempted to make me feel guilty.

"I didn't play you," I defended myself. "Are you okay? What happened?"

"How soon can you get to San Diego General? The shit I have to tell you needs to be done in person," Isaac explained.

"Give me about forty-five minutes," I hung up. I looked at Bailey who was fully dressed. She had opened up her purse, removed a whiskey flask, and taken a long gulp.

"That sounded serious," Bailey growled as the sting of the alcohol set fire to her throat.

"It is," I admitted. I got dressed and drove Bailey back to her car. After we kissed and said goodbye, I told her to drive safely and then headed over to the hospital.

I parked my car and headed towards the emergency door entrance. When I walked in, I saw Isaac filling out paperwork and noticed that his left hand was in a cast. *What the hell?* I quickened my pace.

"What happened?" I pointed to the cast.

"It's been one hell of a night, Jayden." He finished up.

"How did you break your hand?"

"I got involved in bullshit."

"Okay," I said and waited for more information. "Are you in pain?"

"I don't feel a thing, but that's because of the pain killers I am on," Isaac said as we headed toward the exit.

"I don't understand. How did Ava bust you up like that? I mean, I know everyone has a wicked side, but damn. I knew she'd take the news hard, but I could not have ever imagined an outcome like this."

"Ava didn't do this," Isaac said and gestured toward some empty seats at the opposite corner of the room. We walked over and sat down. I gave Isaac my full attention and without my having to ask, he began to tell me what had taken place.

"I told Ava, but I didn't give her details." Isaac pinched the bridge of his nose with the thumb and forefinger of his good hand.

"What does that mean?" I pushed for more details.

"Ava wanted to get to the bottom of my strange behavior. She's got it in her head that I'm having problems at work."

"Why does she think that?"

"Because I didn't correct her and allowed her to assume that's what the problem was." Isaac leaned forward and rested his forearms on his thighs. "She kept pushing and probing until I finally shouted at her to cut me some fucking slack. Ava got really pissed off then and she became physical."

"What?" I was shocked that Ava had stooped to such a level without knowing the truth.

"I deserved it, Jayden. Ava hasn't done anything wrong. She's been a good wife and I know that she'd make a good mother. I just have a need that she is not meeting. I want to be a father. I want a little boy or girl. I want to raise that child with Ava."

"So is that the real reason why you got involved with the young girl? You wanted to start a family?" I asked, delicately probing.

"Probably so," Isaac answered.

"Probably or yes? I'm your friend. There is no need to think one thing, but say something else. We're having real talk. Be honest."

"Yeah. I wanted a child, and somewhere along the way, my anger towards Ava putting off starting a family turned into sullenness. And being seduced by that unpleasantness has led me to this shit here." Isaac held up his hand that was in a cast.

"When was the last time you really sat down and talked this through with Ava?"

"It's been a while. We used to talk about it all of the time. The first excuse was to wait and save money before starting a family. Then her career took off and she didn't want to give that up. As time passed, I began to question whether or not she could conceive. When I asked that question, she took it as an attack on her womanhood, but deep down, I knew that her reaction was a defensive one. I don't think that any woman embraces the idea of not being able to carry a child for her husband. Ava wanted me to understand that she just wasn't ready to raise a family and I wanted her to see that I was. Somehow, this issue has caused us to lose sight of each other."

"Does she truly want children? I'm no medical doctor, but I thought that the risk of having a complicated birth got higher with age. I mean, she isn't getting any younger."

"Ava is thirty seven, so we're still in a good time window," Isaac said.

"Good." I paused and glanced at Isaac. Judging by the look on his face, he was somewhere deep in his mind, analyzing something that either complicated or perplexed him. After an awkward length of silence, I finally asked.

"What is it?"

Isaac smirked painfully before looking directly into my eyes. "I got played." Isaac held on to his next words as if he were holding an explosive. "Big time."

"We all get played. Either we play ourselves or get played by others. The thing is not to get fucked over too badly, I suppose. You knew that you should've strapped up if you were going to play around with Denise." I didn't filter my comment.

"I know that, man!" Isaac raised his voice. "I messed around with Denise out of revenge. I wanted to plant a seed and wave it in Ava's face. The idea was adolescent, I know that, so you don't have to say that to me." Isaac's voice lingered in the air like smoke from a candle that had been snuffed out.

"Flaunting a baby in front of Ava? Dude, that's a crazy way of handling your marital problems. Maybe you guys should get counseling," I suggested.

"We won't need counseling. I'm gonna go home and fix my life. My love for Ava runs deep, and I guess it has taken an ignorant incident like this to make me realize it." Isaac held up his busted hand.

"What's the deal with your hand?"

"Like I said, I got played." Isaac took a deep breath and exhaled long and slowly. "When you didn't show up, I decided to go to see Denise. I had contacted her a while back and we came to an agreement."

"Huh? Wait! Back up. What are you talking about?"

"I reached out to her and told her I would pay her if she stopped pursuing me for child support."

"What? Are you serious? Dude, what is wrong with you?"

"Jayden, I never paid her. I told her that I wanted proof that she had called the dogs off before I started giving her money. Like I said, when you didn't show up, I decided to go pay her an unannounced visit. As I walked up the sidewalk to her apartment, there was a young guy ahead of me. He had on saggy pants that he held up by holding onto his belt buckle. He had on an oversized T-shirt and his hair was braided. He could not have been older than twenty-three or twenty-four, just a kid, from my perspective. It was dark, so he didn't see me, but I could hear him talking on his cell phone clearly.

He said, "Baby, has that nucca started payin' yet? Well, tell him if he don't, we ain't got no damn deal and you is gonna call child services back on his ass. We need to hang that nucca upside down and turn his pockets inside out. Da fool still thinks the baby is his, right? Good. Just keep playin' yo' role like I told ya.'"

"Wait, who was he?" I asked.

"Apparently someone who is a con artist."

"You are fucking bullshitting me."

"I wish I was." Isaac looked at his hand.

"So you got into a fight with the young guy?" I asked.

"No. I came up behind him, positioned myself just right, and cold-cocked him. He went down to the ground. I put my knee on his neck and picked up the phone he was talking on. I said, 'Denise?' and she answered. I told her that I knew everything, and that her little extortion scam wasn't going to work. I told her she could pick her buddy up off the lawn out front. I wanted to fuck him up some more, but when I looked at him, and saw how young he was, I caught myself and realized that I was far too old and smart for that type of bullshit. So, I stood up and I went back to my car. I got in and drove off. That's when I noticed my hand was swelling up."

"That must've been some punch." I sat back for a moment and took in Isaac's account of what had happened. I was both stunned and dumbfounded by the type of people who had entered his life and how his world had been shaken up.

"How and where did you meet Denise?" I asked.

"How and where does a man meet any woman? It just happened. She was young; she made me feel a certain way and I moved forward guided by bitterness and revenge. I made a bad decision; it's just that simple." Isaac stood up and so did I. "I'm going to head on home."

"What are you going to say happened to your hand?"

"I don't know. I'll think of something. Right now, I just want to make up with Ava and put all of this crap behind me. I've been given a second chance and I'm not going to blow it. What about you? What took you so long?"

I smiled wickedly. "I hooked up with the chick from Philly."

"Well, I know this is going to sound really hypocritical, but—"

"Dude," I interrupted him, and we both remained silent. I didn't care to hear a lecture about morals or behavior even though I had just finished offering advice.

"Do your thing, man," Isaac said. I nodded and we both headed out the door.

CHAPTER THIRTY-SEVEN

Bailey

"Oh, Ava, I am so very happy," I gushed.

A blank stare blinked back at me. Ava looked a little unfamiliar, but I couldn't put my finger on what was off about her.

"It's been a while since we've spent time together, so I was checking on you, but seems to me like you're—"

I twirled all the way into my living room.

When I turned and looked at Ava, her face told an interesting story.

"What has gotten into you?" she asked. I looked at her wide eyes and the fake frozen smile plastered across her face. Ava looked lost.

"In the last three weeks, my life has taken such wonderful turn. I'm so happy."

Ava slowly advanced into the living room and dropped her bag onto the sofa.

"If I didn't know any better," Ava started. "I'd think you went and won the doggone lottery or something."

"Girl, something better." I grinned.

One of her unshaped eyebrows rose. Ava pulled her arms up across her chest.

"What the hell could be better than winning the lottery?" she wanted to know.

"A man, Ava! A wonderful, caring, giving man, and I think I love him."

Now Ava's expression changed from amusement to one I'd seen so many times before. She rolled her eyes and gave me a sarcastic look that was all too familiar.

She fell back onto the sofa as if she was bracing herself for a trip down memory lane, or at least down a path we'd been on before.

"Bailey, I thought you were gonna take a break in the men department," she hissed. Ava exhaled as if she couldn't wrap her mind around the conversation we were having.

"When are you gonna learn?" She shook her head, and instantly, I felt the pity she was throwing in my direction.

I shook it all off. "You don't get it, Ava. This guy, he's different. He's sophisticated; he's not young like the rest of those losers who are trying to get over."

But Ava's expression told the whole story. She wasn't buying any of it.

"Don't you remember what happened with Michael? How could you just jump right back into another relationship? This is so irresponsible, Bailey," she admonished.

I stood over her and listened as Ava ran down the list of all the things I did wrong when it came to men: how I was quick to trust; how I rushed to bed; and how I took irresponsible, unnecessary chances when I didn't have to.

"It's why you can't get that husband you want, Bailey. No man wants it easy. If he knows he can come to you and get it without the least bit of struggle, guess what he's gonna do?"

My eyes fixed on hers. Her words might as well have been made of rubber. They simply bounced off of me.

"Bailey, do you hear what I'm trying to tell you?" she asked.

I grinned so hard, I know she probably thought I was losing my mind.

"Bailey, we've talked about this over and over and over again. You can't keep doing the exact same thing, in the same way, and then acting lost and confused when you get the same damn results." She shook her head.

There was that pity again.

"How do you expect to get a husband if you keep hopping in and out of beds, with no regard whatsoever to what that's going to do—"

"Ava, enough," I said quietly.

She looked at me again like she thought I might have been possessed by a ghost or something.

I walked closer and sat next to her on the sofa.

"I don't think you understand," I began. "My focus has changed completely. And what I'm trying to tell you is, these last few weeks with my new man have been some of the very best. I was focusing on all the wrong things before."

"So, this new mystery man, he's all of that and then some?" Ava asked curtly.

"You know what? Let's not talk about him anymore. How's Isaac? How are the two of you?"

When a dark gloom washed over her face, my heart started to race.

"Oh, Ava, is everything okay?"

Suddenly my happiness didn't seem all that important. Ava was always hard on me, but she'd been that way since we were younger. I had grown to expect her criticism and I learned not to take any of it personally. The pain I saw in her eyes made me feel bad.

Here I was going on and on about my happiness and my new

man, when I didn't even take a moment to realize that Ava was going through something of her own.

"Is everything okay with Isaac? What happened? What's wrong?" I asked.

Were those tears in her eyes?

"Ava, what's going on?"

"Bailey, just know that marriage is a lot of hard, hard work."

I wasn't going to keep begging her to tell me what was going on. I pulled back a little and looked at her.

"I don't want to talk about me and my problems." Ava sniffled a little. "So, now tell me about this new man of yours. Who is he and where'd you meet him?"

I just looked at her. So she expected me to spill all the details about my business, but when it came to her and whatever was going on with Isaac, that was top secret?

"Well, let's just say he makes me very happy and I do the same for him. Despite what you think, we have taken it slow. We've traveled together, and had a great time and nothing happened. He's been there for me when I needed him most, but you know what, I don't want to jinx what we have. Just know that I can't remember a time when I've been happier. Ava, for me, this is a great place and I have a great feeling about him."

"Well, I'm happy for you," Ava finally said.

"You should be. He really does make me happy, and after all I've been through, I think we can both agree that I deserve a little bit of happiness."

"You do, Bailey. And don't take my questions for anything but what they are—me being concerned that you're making the best choices, that's all."

"Ava, it really doesn't matter. I think I've been putting too much thought into it. Right now, I'm simply going with the flow. My new relationship started out as a friendship, and it has blossomed into something real nice. I think we're gonna be just fine." I rose from the couch. I slapped my hands together and said, "Now let me fix you this new drink I had. You're gonna love it!"

CHAPTER THIRTY-EIGHT

Ava

This situation with Isaac had me questioning everything. It was one thing to question what you didn't know, but to be so uncertain that you start questioning the things you've always known to be true made me wonder whether we'd be able to bounce back.

I thought about all of the advice I had given Bailey over the years, and felt like such a fraud. When Sylvia called to talk to me, I barely had the energy to hold up my end of our conversation.

"How did I not know what he was doing?"

"What are you talking about, Ava?" Sylvia asked.

"Oh, girl, I'm sorry. My mind was somewhere else. I was thinking out loud."

I wished it was as easy as shaking the thoughts from my mind, but there were so many emotions all wrapped up in what I was going through. I didn't know what would happen with Isaac and me.

Sylvia went on about some incident at work, and all I could do was think about the strange things that had been happening with Isaac.

Was I just as dumb as Bailey? How did I not suspect he had been up to something? I thought his struggle was over work, not another woman. I made the mistake of thinking I knew my man better than I knew myself, and it was obvious I didn't.

"So you might be called into the deposition," Sylvia said.

"Oh. Okay, well, just let me know what you need me to do."

"Ava, you're not listening to a single word I'm telling you!"

"Okay, okay. I'm sorry. You're right. I've got a lot on my mind. What's up? What's going on?"

"You know what, forget about the work stuff. Girl. What the hell is going on with you? What's up with Isaac?" she asked.

That was the million-dollar question. Everyone wanted to know what was up with Isaac. The truth was, I wanted to know what was up with Isaac, too.

"I don't even like the way you're sounding. Hold on a sec," Sylvia said.

I listened as she spoke in the background.

"Jayden!" she yelled. "Hey, I'm about to go over to Ava's. Call if you need something."

I wanted to tell Sylvia she didn't need to come over, but once she'd made up her mind, it was hard to talk any sense into her. She came back to the phone.

"You eaten yet?"

"Not in much of a mood to eat," I said.

"Girl, you sound a mess. I'll be right over. Where's Isaac anyway?"

"He's upstairs. You know he's still on those pain pills, so he's laid up in front of his big screen. You know men can't handle any kind of pain."

"If that ain't the truth, I don't know what is. Okay, I'll see you soon."

"Sylvia, I'm okay, girl. Don't stress yourself. I'll be fine," I tried to tell her. But by the time I tried to plead my case, the call had ended.

I heard footsteps moving around upstairs, but I wasn't the least bit interested in checking in on Isaac. I wondered whether the faith would ever return to my marriage.

I walked around the family room and picked up a bowl, a couple of glasses, and an empty water bottle. I straightened out the pillows and sprayed the Hawaiian Breeze air freshener to get rid of the stale scent that lingered in the air. Once the place was straightened up, I turned the ceiling fan on low and stepped into the guest bathroom.

"I don't know how this house gets so dirty and it's only two people living here," I muttered, as I searched for cleaning products under the sink.

After a quick sprucing job in the guest bathroom, I pulled fresh hand towels from the laundry room, and sprayed air freshener in the bathroom too.

Satisfied the house was company ready, I walked back to the family room and turned the TV to OWN.

"Ava?" Isaac's drugged voice called out to me.

Would it be wrong for me to act like I didn't hear him?

"A-aava?"

I got up from the recliner and walked to the bottom of the staircase. I looked up and answered my husband.

"Yeah?"

"Can you bring me a glass of water, please?"

I rolled my eyes. I was relieved when the doorbell rang. I turned toward the door and he asked, "You expecting somebody?"

"Yeah. Sylvia. I'll bring your water up in a sec," I said.

"Okay, thanks, babe." Isaac turned and walked back toward the upstairs game room.

"Coming," I sang as I walked toward the front door. I needed to get my game face ready. I knew Sylvia wouldn't rest until she was able to wrangle every single detail about Isaac's indiscretion out of me. I inhaled and jerked the front door open. The fake smile dropped from my face.

"Hey, gir—" The words caught in my throat as my face twisted in confusion.

"Hi. You don't know me, but I think we need to talk," the very pregnant young woman who stood on my doorstep said.

My heart took an instant nosedive.

"You're Ava. You're Isaac's wife, right?"

I looked around outside. I wanted her to be at the wrong address, but it registered in my brain that she wouldn't know my husband's or my name if she was at the wrong address.

My gaze fell to her swollen belly, and she took a hand and placed it atop her stomach. She rubbed her hand over the top of it as if to let me know it was real.

"Uh, who wants to know?"

Those were the only words my voice could find. There were so many other questions I wanted to ask, but that was what tumbled from my lips. I was lost.

"Hey, Ava, what's going on here?" Sylvia walked up just in time. She looked at the stranger, down at her belly, then squeezed past the girl and into my doorway.

Sylvia looked at her, then back at me.

"Ava, who's this?" she asked me.

"She just walked up, not even a minute before you. I thought it was you at the door."

Sylvia looked at the girl, "Hey, umm, what can we do for you?"

"Oh, my name is Denise."

Her name didn't mean a thing to Sylvia or me. We stood and waited for the rest, but what happened next threw everything into a complete tailspin.

"Ooooh!" Denise hollered. We all looked down at the gush of fluid on my doorstep.

The girl cried, "Oh my God! Please, not here! Not here! My water just broke!" She let out a gut-wrenching cry and stumbled back a bit.

"Oh, shit!" Sylvia yelled. "Denise, are you having your baby now?"

The piercing squeal was her only answer, and it had rendered me motionless. I could hardly breathe.

CHAPTER THIRTY-NINE

Jayden

The moment Sylvia pulled out of the driveway I was happier than a dog with two tails. I got comfortable and called Bailey.

"Hey, daddy."

"What's up, hot stuff?" I smiled and then laughed deeply.

"Oooh, that's the type of sound that makes me wanna rest on my back and open my legs for you," she said.

"I'm glad you're in that type of mood. I was thinking about hooking up today."

"How much time do you have?"

"It doesn't matter, baby. All you need to know is that I ache for you. I need you to meet me so that you can scratch this unquenchable itch that I have." I was in lust and had no desire to lasso the feeling or give additional thought to what I was doing.

"Where is your wife?" Bailey asked.

"Off with her girlfriend again."

"Damn, your wife must be the dumbest bitch on the planet. There is no way in hell I would spend as much time as she does with her girlfriend, especially if I had a man like you at home. Seriously, if you were my man, I would make you my priority and we would work on creating a lifetime of bliss." Bailey seemed more irritated and aggressive than usual. For a brief moment, I heard a soft voice in my mind warn me, but I ignored it and heard what I wanted to hear.

"Now see, I like the sound of that. You're the type of woman who seems to know how to cater to a man," I wondered what type of life I could have with Bailey.

"You're damn right I know how to cater to man. Shit, what you have experienced with me over the past few weeks is just the surface of much deeper waters."

"Is that right?" I allowed her comment to walk around freely in my mind and knock down mental pillars of marital contentment that had stood for decades.

"Baby, if you wanna see just how deeply my passion goes, you have got to make some serious moves." Bailey's comment was direct and clear. I sensed that she was pulling for a decisive action on my part.

"What are you talking about?" I asked, for absolute clarity.

"Leave her. It's obvious that there is something seriously wrong with your marriage. If everything was blissful, our relationship wouldn't be as strong as it is. Besides, it's not like she has you weighed down with a bunch of small children."

Bailey's comment caused an uncharacteristic paralysis in me. For a moment, I mulled over the status of my wounded marriage.

"You have a point there." I looked around the house and all that was in it. Every object suddenly represented the squandered history of the life I shared with Sylvia.

"Of course I have a point. Think about it, Jayden. Why are you really there if you don't want to be? When are you going to leave that sham you call a marriage? What's really holding you back? It's not kids or some type of financial situation. You've told me already that if you wanted to leave, you could do it any time you wanted to. Why haven't you found the courage to do what you've wanted to do for a long time?"

"Are you calling me a coward? Are you picking a fight with me?" I raised my voice. I thought she had forwarded an invitation to a verbal brawl and I began to lace up my gloves.

"I would never do that, baby." Bailey finally broke the silence that hung between us. "All I want is a real shot at showing you just how good I can be to you. We can do all types exciting things together, Jayden. We both have strong incomes and we don't have little children to consider. We could travel within the States and abroad and dine at five-star restaurants. We could make love all the time, anyway you want it. I want to fully submit to you, daddy. I want to have all of you and not just part of you. Deep down, baby, I know you want the same thing. I know you want me. All you have to do is take that first step towards my welcoming arms."

"Bailey."

"Yes, daddy?"

"Slow down." I felt as if I was being operated on without an anesthetic. "How long have you had thoughts like that in your head?" I asked.

"Daddy, all you need to know is that I'm willing to do anything, and I do mean anything, to prove to you that I am what you've been craving."

I paused, finding myself caught up in Bailey's suggestion. It was a seductive one that filled my mind with images and visions of how much more satisfying my life could be.

"And as far as sex goes, I am not the type of woman who would tell you no. I'll give it to you whenever and however you want it. I would never become boring in bed." Bailey paused, and silence hung in the air. Somehow she had studied me without my knowledge, and had gotten around my mental defenses. I needed a moment to process the logical, but crazy, notion that had just been infused into my mind. I heard a tone come through the phone and realized that Isaac was calling. I welcomed the distraction.

"Bailey, baby, let me call you back. My son is trying to reach me," I lied.

"Okay, daddy, no problem. Call me when you're done, and I'll make myself available to you in any way you want or need." She made a kissing sound and then hung up. I exhaled before I took Isaac's call.

"Jayden, this shit is fucked up and I don't know what to do! What should I do, man?" I had never heard Isaac in such a panic before. The words rushed out of his mouth almost faster than he could form them. He sounded as if he had just inadvertently committed a homicide.

"Yo, man, calm the fuck down." I shifted my mental focus from Bailey's thoughts to Isaac's situation. "What the hell are you talking about?" I asked, matching his intensity with my own.

"Denise is here, man, and she is having the baby in the foyer of my house!"

"What the fuck did you just say?"

"Denise is here! Ava and Sylvia brought her into the house when her water broke! I'm pacing back and forth in the upstairs bathroom, man, and I don't know what to do!"

"How in the hell did she find out where you lived?" I asked. Although Isaac's situation wasn't something I had been involved in, at least not directly, my loyalty to him as a friend dictated that I share his torment.

"I don't have a clue as to how she fucking found me. Maybe she looked at my identification, and found wrote down my address during one of our rendezvous. I thought this shit was over and behind me, man! This shit wasn't supposed to come to my fucking doorstep!" I could hear the anxiety in Isaac's voice.

"Isaac, take it easy. Tell me exactly what's going on." I tried to remain calm.

"Isaac! Have you called nine-one-one like I asked you to? And where are the towels I told you to bring?" I heard Ava shout out from somewhere in the background.

"I'll be there in a minute, damn!" Isaac barked back. "Game over! This shit is so fucked up! Fucked up! Fucked up!" Isaac kept repeating himself as if his mind had snapped.

"Dude, call for help."

"I want her out of my house, Jayden. This is my home!" I realized that Isaac was unwilling to accept the predicament he found himself in.

"Have you thought about praying?" I thought Isaac was having a mental breakdown.

"Praying?" Isaac repeated the word as if it were a derogatory term.

"Are you on the phone with the nine-one-one operator?" I heard Ava who seemed very close to him now.

"No, I'm talking to Jayden," Isaac said.

"Jayden?" I heard a confused and bewildered tone in Ava's voice.

"Yeah." Isaac sounded totally lost, like a ship trying to navigate through a thick fog without a chart or navigation system.

"I don't have time for your stupidity right now. Sylvia and I are going to drive this girl to the hospital. We'll get there before the paramedics get here."

"Who is she?" I heard Isaac ask Ava as if Denise were a complete and total stranger.

"She said that her name is Denise and apparently she knows both of us by name. I'm gonna get to the bottom of this shit today, Isaac," I could hear Ava's voice quake. "My spirit is telling me that light has just been shed on your dark secret, you son of a bitch!"

"Ava! We've got to go now!" I heard Sylvia's voice shout out from farther away.

"Jayden—" I could tell that an emotional boulder had lodged in Isaac's throat.

"Go to the hospital, Isaac. I'll meet you there," I said, and hung up the phone. I put my cell phone down and exhaled as I combed my fingers through my hair. I was about to head toward the bathroom when my cell phone buzzed twice, indicating that a text message had arrived. I looked at it and saw that it was from Bailey.

Will catch up with you later, something big has come up and my best friend really needs me right now.

CHAPTER FORTY

Bailey

When I pulled up at Ava and Isaac's house, there was mad chaos underway. I wasn't sure what to do. There was screaming, loud voices, and much more.

The door was wide open and it looked like a woman was lying on the foyer floor. I was nervous as I walked up. I wasn't sure what was going on, but I suspected that Ava didn't realize she had butt dialed me.

At first I thought she was trying to get me to listen to something, but when I heard the rambling in the background about water breaking and cursing, I felt like my girl was in trouble. I was close to her place anyway, so it was nothing for me to do a quick drive-by.

"Ava, w-w-w-what the hell is going on here?" I stepped into the house.

All eyes turned to me. A woman lay on the floor with her legs gapped wide open, and she was in labor. Sylvia, Ava's other friend, looked like a madwoman about to perform surgery, and Isaac paced back and forth with the phone glued to the side of his head.

I stood frozen. I had never seen the woman on the floor before and didn't understand why she had chosen Ava's house to give birth.

"Ava," I called out again. "Who is this and what's happening?"

"She just showed up and went into labor," Ava said.

My eyes grew wide. *What did she mean, she just showed up?*

"The ambulance is on the way," Ava told me.

"No. We can't wait." Sylvia jumped to her feet. "We need to go. She's about to have this baby right here. We can't wait for the paramedics," she insisted.

"Bailey, you drove here, right?" Ava asked.

"Umm, yeah, I did. Why?"

"We may need you to drive us to the hospital. This woman is about to have her baby and I don't want her to have it here," Ava said.

I glanced down at the woman. She had been squirming and hollering the whole time I was there. She clutched on to Ava's hand as Sylvia barked orders down near the woman's legs.

"We're not gonna make it if we don't leave now!" Sylvia screamed.

"We? Who is she and what's she doing here?"

"Her name is Denise."

The way Ava said the woman's name, it made me wonder if these three had been friends all along, and I simply wasn't aware. I didn't know this chick and I damn sure didn't want her screwing up my car by giving birth inside of it.

"Is there an emergency here?" a voice near the door asked.

I had never been so happy to see San Diego firefighters before.

"Oh, yes, she's gone into labor," Sylvia volunteered.

"Okay, okay. We've got it from here," the man said.

We watched as the EMT worker and his partner kneeled down next to Denise.

"It's going to be okay. We've got you; you'll be fine," the paramedic said.

Ava, Sylvia, Isaac, and I stood off to the side as the workers focused on Denise.

As they coached her through labor, she looked over at Isaac and started to cry.

"I'm so sorry," she sobbed.

"C'mon. Let's focus. This baby isn't gonna wait," the paramedic said. "You can apologize later. On three, I want you to give me a real good push," he said.

"What is she saying sorry about?" I asked Ava without thinking. All eyes locked on me as if I had just asked the most retarded question ever. My eyes wandered from Ava, to Sylvia, and then to Isaac, who looked like the cat who'd just swallowed a rat.

I frowned and fixed my gaze on Ava. *I just knew this pregnant chick on the floor didn't have anything to do with her husband. What would her precious saint-like Sylvia have to say about this?*

"Ava, who is this chick?" I asked.

"Yeah. Who is this chick?" Ava asked in Isaac's direction.

"We need to get her to a hospital!" one of the paramedics said.

"Oh, God!" Denise cried. She reached out and clutched on to Sylvia's hand. I was very confused, but I wasn't about to ask another question.

"Ma'am, you coming with her?" the paramedic asked Sylvia.

"Uh, yeah. I guess so."

Isaac stepped up. "Here, Sylvia. I'll follow behind you guys so you'll have a ride back."

My eyebrows inched up. I didn't know what the hell was going on. But I figured some alone time with Ava would help straighten things out. Ava stood off to the side but she never offered to lift a finger.

We watched as the paramedics loaded Denise's gurney into the back of their ambulance. Sylvia hopped up and got inside. Isaac rushed to his car, and took off right behind the ambulance.

I didn't wait for them to make the corner before I turned my focus to Ava.

"What the hell was that about?" I asked.

Ava looked at me with sad eyes for a long time before she spoke. She took a deep breath and motioned for me to follow her. I walked next to her back into the house, and we looked at the mess at her front door and foyer.

"It smells like shit in here," she said.

It smelled like shit for sure, but she had some explaining to do. After enduring all of her lectures about making choices and all the relationship counseling, I needed to understand why some chick was giving birth on her floor.

"I think Isaac done fucked up," Ava said simply.

I was speechless. I stood at a complete loss for words.

"You trying to say that girl is having your husband's baby?"

Ava shook her head. I followed her to the kitchen where she dug under the kitchen sink. She pulled out a small, black bucket and a ton of cleaning products.

"I don't know what I'm trying to say. All I know is she showed up with a story to tell, but went into labor before she could spill the beans."

"This is too much."

When my phone rang, I contemplated not answering, but figured what the hell.

"Hello?"

Ava began to clean her nemesis' bodily fluids from the floor, and I focused on my call.

"Hey, baby. No. Like I told you earlier, my friend needed me, so I'm sitting here with her now," I cooed into the phone.

I looked at Ava as she worked.

"I won't be here long. When will you be free?" I asked him.

I giggled at his answer. "Jayden, you need to quit. Jayden," I cooed again.

When I turned to see a bewildered expression on Ava's face, I stopped talking. "Jayden, honey, let me call you when I leave here."

"Did you just say Jayden?" Ava asked.

CHAPTER FORTY-ONE

Ava

I couldn't take any damn more! There, I said it. I was ready to throw in the damn towel. My head wasn't finished spinning from the pregnant woman who showed up on my doorstep, and now I heard Bailey giggling and sweet talking on the phone with my best friend's husband?

"Bailey, is your new man married?" I asked.

My heartbeat thumped loudly in my ears as I waited for her to confirm my fear.

"Oh. I know good and well you're not trying to judge me when your man just rushed off to the hospital with some pregnant chick who was close to giving birth in your damn house," Bailey said. "And last I checked, you ain't never said nothing about a damn surrogate."

What could I say to Bailey? She had a point. With all that was on my plate, the last thing I needed was more problems to worry about.

I got up from my spot and grabbed the bucket. As I was about to walk toward the back of the house, Bailey called out to me.

"Ava, I'm sorry. I didn't mean that. It's just I purposely avoided saying anything to you about Jayden. I didn't want to hear anything about how wrong what I'm doing is," she said.

"What's wrong with it?"

"Ava. Jayden is married." She had the nerve to hang her head low. I was so mad at Bailey in that moment. To me, she was no different than the skeezer who showed up on my doorstep with information to share with me.

"Yeah, I know," I said, and walked away from her.

"Wait, what do you mean you know? Up until now, you didn't even know his name. How do you all of a sudden know everything there is to know about him?"

"Bailey, I've only met two people named Jayden in my entire life. One was during my senior trip in high school, and the other is my best friend's husband," she said.

The look on Bailey's face told me she was completely stunned by the news I had just delivered. But why should I be the only one to swallow a massive pill today?

I wasn't in the kitchen for two seconds before Bailey came rushing in there. I washed my hands at the sink and wondered why she showed up at my house any way.

"That's not funny," Bailey said as she moved in my direction.

"Funny is the very last thing on my mind right now. Is it possible that you could be with another man named Jayden? Of course, that's possible. But I can show you pictures of Sylvia's husband and we can see just how much of a coincidence this really is," I said.

Bailey motioned for me to stop. She shook her head.

"I knew he was married, but when we were in Philly together, he made me feel so important, so special. After all I went through with Michael, it felt good to have a man interested in me. Jayden is a good man. We didn't set out to hook up. As a matter of fact, when we were in Philly, nothing even went down. It wasn't until we got back and he helped me out a few times that we got close and one thing led to another."

Bailey shrugged like that was supposed to excuse her behavior. She was selfish and naive. She didn't even stop to think about the consequences of screwing another woman's husband. Not to mention, the awkward position she'd put me in.

I rolled my eyes at her and the foolishness. I wondered whether Isaac had also made his female friend feel special. I guess she felt so damn special, she had to come and rub my face in it.

"I don't expect you to understand," she said.

When Bailey started picking at her nail beds, I wondered what the hell she must've been thinking to start carrying on with some married man.

"He's not leaving Sylvia. I don't care what he's told you, or what he tells you. He's not leaving her," I said adamantly.

"You don't know what Jayden, or any other man, is gonna do. I don't mean to keep pointing at the situation I walked up on, but I think I can safely say that neither you, Sylvia, or even I would know what a man's gonna do. Earlier, Jayden and I were talking about a future together, our future," she said.

I couldn't remember a time when I had seen Bailey so defiant and confident. How did I not know she had been screwing my best friend's husband? Could I have been that caught up in the drama going on with Isaac and me that I was oblivious to what was happening around me?

Instantly, my mind started to think about the times Bailey talked about her new man. I guess the joke was on me. I thought this joker was just another sucker who would leave her brokenhearted and alone.

Never in a million years would I have guessed that joker was Sylvia's husband.

"Wow. I can't believe Jayden's married to Sylvia. I wonder how she's gonna feel when she realizes I'm the one who took her man? I'll bet she won't be talking all crazy about me anymore," Bailey said.

I frowned.

"What's that supposed to mean?"

Bailey twisted her pursed lips to one side and gave me a knowing glance. "You must really think I'm stupid, huh? You think I didn't know how she felt about me? The woman looked down her nose at me every chance she got. And who knows how many times I've been the topic of discussion as you two went to happy hour or dinner. But that's okay. While she was busy minding my business, she wasn't minding her own, and now, I've got her man."

"Bailey! So, you're not gonna stop seeing him?" I asked.

"Jayden comes to life around me. We are good for each other and I know I can make him a better wife than Sylvia," Bailey said.

"Oh my God," I muttered.

"God ain't got nothing to do with this. Listen, I'm about to go. I'm supposed to meet Jayden later for a drink. I'll check on you afterwards."

For a long time after Bailey left, I stood there and wondered what the hell was happening to the world as I thought I knew it.

CHAPTER FORTY-TWO

Jayden

When I arrived at the hospital, I called Isaac. He told me that he and Sylvia were allowed into the maternity ward since they came in with Denise, and that Ava was back at home with another girlfriend. I asked one of the guards at the desk to direct me to the ward, but he stopped me. I only knew Denise's first name and I wasn't related to her. I called Isaac back and told him that I would wait for him and Sylvia in the lobby. Thirty minutes later, they both exited an elevator and walked towards me. I gave Sylvia a hug and kiss on the cheek and looked into Isaac's disorientated eyes.

"What happened?" I asked him.

"She had a boy. Seven pounds and eight ounces; he's a beautiful baby." Isaac smiled painfully.

"What did she name him?" I asked.

"Isaac Jr.," Sylvia answered for him. My eyes began to play tennis between Isaac and my wife.

"She knows, man. There is no sense in trying to run away from my mess. I have owned up to it." Isaac looked like he'd just been in a prize fight with the heavyweight champion. The turmoil that he felt on the inside was written all over his face, body posture, and the tone of his voice. His shoulders were slumped; his eyes were puffy and he was breathless, as if something from deep within had a choke hold on him.

"I made them do a DNA test," Sylvia interjected. "Denise claims that it's Isaac's baby, but Isaac told me how he believes it belongs to some other dude. The results will be available in about three days. Then, he'll know for sure if the baby is his." Sylvia glanced at Isaac and gave him a deeply disappointed glare.

"The baby is probably not yours," I said as I reached out to touch Isaac's shoulder. I wanted to comfort him in any way that I could, but Isaac seemed distant. He found a seat and slumped down in it.

"How could you do this to Ava, Isaac? How could you ruin everything that you guys have built together?" Sylvia asked gut-busting questions that were painful for Isaac to answer.

"I wanted children, Sylvia, and Ava…" Isaac didn't finish his thought.

"I hope Denise was worth all of this pain and drama." Sylvia stopped interrogating him and moved away. Isaac and I both knew that no matter how much explaining he did, Sylvia would never fully understand that Isaac behaved badly due to a deep need was not being met by Ava.

"Is the baby healthy?" I asked.

"Yes. He has soft skin and pretty, curly, black hair. I put my pinkie finger in his and he wrapped his tiny little hand around it." Isaac paused, and buried his face in the palms of his hands. "Dear God, what have I done?"

"You've fucked up is what you've done." Sylvia walked back over without an ounce sympathy for Isaac. "You're going to go back home and explain everything to Ava. You're going to tell her what you did, how you did it, and why you did it. She deserves to know, Isaac."

"She sort of already knows, right?" I asked. Sylvia shot daggers at me with her eyes when I asked that question.

"Ava is not stupid, but he needs to face her and explain why," Sylvia continued. "So come on; let's go back to your house, Isaac, so that I can get my car and you can do the reasonable thing."

I arrived back at Isaac's house and when I stepped inside, my sinuses were attacked by the scent of cleaning products. Sylvia called out Ava's name and she answered. She was in the kitchen. Sylvia was about to go see her, but I grabbed her.

"We should go," I said. "This is something that they need to work out."

Sylvia glared at me as if I had two heads. She was emotionally cocked, and I sensed that she was so close to Ava, that she felt Ava's heartache, rage, and bitterness just as strongly as Ava did. "My best friend has been devastated by this. The least I can do is ask if there is anything I can do to help her." The amount of venom in Sylvia's voice was at a level that I had never heard before.

"Baby, we shouldn't go in there. This is none of our business," I spoke more assertively.

"Whatever, Jayden." Sylvia jerked away from me and moved towards the kitchen. Isaac, who stood next to me, took a few deep breaths and headed into the kitchen behind Sylvia. I was about to follow him when my phone rang. It was Bailey. I was about to step back outside and answer her call when I heard Sylvia scream out my name as if someone was holding her at gunpoint. I rushed into the kitchen to see what was going on and saw Sylvia standing near the sink with flames of contempt ablaze in her eyes.

"What's going on?" I asked, confused as to why Sylvia was so filled with rage and fury.

"Just back up, man," Isaac warned me.

"What?" I was confused.

"You've been fucking that whore Bailey behind my back!" Sylvia screamed at me. I looked into the eyes of everyone in the room and realized that everyone's secret was exposed. I looked at Isaac and wondered if the bastard had betrayed me. The truth hung violently in the air like a kite caught in a hurricane.

"What are you talking about?" I got defensive and started the process of denying the accusation.

"Really, Jayden," Ava said. "Bailey was just here. She's a friend of mine. I've known her for years."

"Fuck," I said as I connected all of the dots. I was frozen. The moment seemed surreal. I felt as if I had disappeared and was no longer in the room. There was only silence. I didn't see or hear anything. Suddenly, I saw a flash of white light. When my vision came back, I had an annoying and loud ringing sound in my ear. My legs have given out and Isaac helped me to remain steady.

"You son of bitch!" I heard Sylvia snarling at me. I looked at her and saw that she had a black, iron skillet in her hand. She must've grabbed it from the rack.

"You hit me?" I asked, stunned that Sylvia had responded violently. Sylvia rushed out of the kitchen and out of the house.

"Sylvia!" I hollered her name as I stumbled after her. She got into her car and locked the door. "Let's talk about this." I pleaded with her.

"Get the fuck away from me!" she moaned angrily as she cranked up the car.

"You're not leaving until we talk about this." I noticed blood splattering on the ground around me. I touched my head, and looked at my fingers that were covered in my blood.

"I gave you everything, mother fucker!"

"We need to talk!" I yelled at her as I slapped my bloody hand against the window. I wanted to somehow, someway, reconcile the pain I had caused. Sylvia made the car engine roar like a wild beast. I moved and stood behind the car with my hands held up, pleading with her to stay. Sylvia, in a moment of emotional insanity, backed up and nailed me. I felt myself flying through the air and when I landed, I heard the hollowed sound of my body and head slam against the concrete.

I opened my eyes, but my vision was blurry. I blinked a few times until my eyes came into focus. My body ached all over. I noticed that my arm was in a cast from my shoulder to my wrist. I groaned as I tried to reposition myself. The scent wafting through the air confirmed that I was in the hospital. I looked around the room expecting to find Sylvia, but was surprised when I saw Bailey.

"Hey, how are you feeling?" She walked over so that I could see her better.

"Water," I whispered. My throat was dry.

"There are some ice chips here," Bailey said. She picked up the cup, placed it to my mouth, and tipped it just enough to get the ice chips past my lips. I sucked on them until my throat felt better.

"Sylvia fucked you up real good. If I had been there, she would have had to go through me to get to you." I suddenly found Bailey to be emotionally draining. My mind was in such a fog and I didn't know what to say or think. I was befuddled and afraid like a pitiful dog that hides when it hears the growl of thunder.

"How long have I been here?" I asked.

"Four days," she said.

Damn, I thought to myself.

"I can't stay long. I'm on lunch and since the hospital is close, I have been checking in on you."

"What happened?" I asked.

"A lot of complicated shit," Bailey answered as she looked into my eyes and stroked my hair. "You'll be okay. though. I tried to call and warn you that Ava knew about us, and that she wasn't going to keep our affair a secret. Ava has a big mouth, and Sylvia has an evil side that no one had ever seen until four days ago. From what Ava has told me, she really lost it. Then she tried to give me a lecture about leaving you alone, but I told her that she didn't understand how in love we are. When you get out of here, you need to come stay with me so I can take care of you." She smiled, then leaned in and kissed my lips.

"Where is Sylvia?" I asked.

"Who gives a shit!" Bailey snapped. "The bitch should be in jail for attempted homicide. She doesn't matter anymore. We're no longer a secret. We can move forward with our lives now, daddy. Don't you see that? We are going to be so happy now." I looked into Bailey's eyes and was speechless. My thoughts were trapped somewhere between misery and trepidation.

"I know of a really good attorney we can use. Once he finds out that Sylvia ran you over with her car, I'm positive he can expedite your divorce." Bailey stood up, looked down at me and smiled sweetly. "Oh, and just so that you know, Isaac's DNA test came back and it wasn't his baby. And another thing you should know, Sylvia hasn't been here to see you, not even once. Ava told me that she's staying with her mother. Apparently, she can't stand being in the house any longer." A delighted smile formed across Bailey's lips.

"I won," she said, "I finally won. I would have loved to have been there when Ava told Sylvia that I was fucking you. I bet the look on her face was priceless." Bailey paused, and then laughed. She kissed me once more. "I'll be back tonight after work, baby." Bailey winked at me and walked out.

CHAPTER FORTY-THREE

Bailey

Two weeks had passed and I hadn't heard anything about Jayden or from him. As I worked on the specs for office space for a new client, my mind kept wandering to thoughts of what in the hell must be going on. I twirled the pencil between my fingers and went back to the last time I went to check on him. When my mind went back there, the memory felt like it had just happened moments ago.

That day, I'd rushed into the hospital room, and ran back outside to check the number on the side of the door. The number hadn't changed, but the name above it was gone.

"Ma'am? Are you okay? Can I help you with something?" a nurse had asked.

"This room. Errr, it's empty. Where's the—I mean he was just here last night," I stammered.

"Oh, you must be talking about Jayden Henner. His wife came and they left earlier," she said.

I swallowed the bile that threatened to rise in my throat. Suddenly, I felt hot and cold at the same time. The nurse's bright eyes grew wide. The smile slowly faded from her face and her features twisted into a frown.

"Ma'am? Are you gonna be okay? Are you family? Is there something wrong? Are you hurt?"

How could I say yes, my heart aches once again? I staggered to the wall and held myself up by leaning against it. The nurse moved closer to me and grabbed my arm as if to try and steady me.

"Do you need some water? Here, why don't we get you some place to sit," she offered.

"I'm fine. Really. Thank you. I just felt a little lightheaded, but I'm good."

I straightened myself where I stood and adjusted my clothes. I looked at the blank name card above the room number and pulled out my cell phone.

A tall man wearing a lab coat slowed as he passed us. "Everything okay here, Evelyn?"

"Yes. This lady, she was a little wobbly, but says she's feeling okay."

The doctor looked at me, and I nodded and forced a smile to my face. "Yes. I am good, really. I need to figure out where my brother is," I said and showed the phone as if to prove I really was okay.

Outside in the parking lot, I leaned up against my car for strength.

"He got back with her? She tried to kill his ass and he went back to her?" I asked myself in disbelief.

I looked around the parking lot, unlocked my door, and slipped inside. Words could hardly express how stunned I was by this. Then, it hit me.

"Oh shit! What if she came and forced him to go with her?" That had to be it. Nothing else made sense. A flash of adrenaline rushed through my veins as I dialed Jayden's number yet again.

By the time I had called the fifth time and there was no answer, I still wasn't convinced that he hadn't been kidnapped by his wife.

"Ava!" I screamed.

I jumped into my car and raced to Ava's house. I understood that I would probably be the last person she wanted to see, but the truth was I wasn't too happy with her either. She basically showed me where her loyalty stood.

She chose to tell Sylvia my business, versus keeping my secret. Ava had drawn the line in the sand, and I was about to go and cross it.

When I saw both her car and Isaac's, my bravado seemed to fade just a little. I knew they were in the midst of their own personal storm, but Ava should've thought about that shit before she went running her mouth to her girl about me!

My moment of concern didn't last too long. I turned off the car and hopped out. I advanced up the walkway that led to their front door and knocked on the door like someone behind it owed me money.

"Coming," Ava said.

When she pulled the front door open, I could tell she hadn't been expecting me. But I didn't care.

"Haven't you caused enough problems?" she greeted me.

"Ava, I'm not here for a fight. I know you don't approve of my relationship with Jayden, but we are going to be together. Sylvia is the past."

She snickered and tossed me a nasty look. Ava pulled the door closed as if she didn't want me peeking inside her house.

"You're nothing but a worthless homewrecker. I knew you were stupid before when it came to men, but this takes the cake," she said.

"Oh, so now I'm stupid? I'm stupid because I met and fell in love with a wonderful man who is sick and tired of his stale marriage?"

"You don't get it, do you?" Ava asked.

I looked at her with defiance across my face. "Has it ever crossed your mind that maybe it's you and your girl Sylvia who don't get it?" My weight fell back onto one hip as I waited for her answer. I tossed a hand to my hip as I waited for Ava to ponder her answer.

She frowned again.

This time, she shook her head slowly.

"I don't need your pity anymore," I said. "You see, for years, I guess, I've been the center of discussion for the two married women. Poor Bailey, she wants a man and can't keep one; poor Bailey, she's desperate for a husband and can't get one." I snickered. "I'll bet the two of you probably laughed at me over drinks. Didn't you two have a standing happy hour at least once or twice a month? Well, I guess the joke is on the two of you. Poor Bailey got herself a man and a husband!" I started cracking up.

Ava clutched to that door tightly, and I could see the veins at her temple throbbing.

"Whooo-hooo, and the clincher here is that the husband I got belongs to one of the two most self-righteous, holier-than-thou wives who thought their shit didn't stink!"

"Bailey! What's your problem? No one has been out to get you. I'm glad you found your knight in shining armor. I just wish it wasn't my best friend's husband! Or anyone's husband for that matter."

"Ava, where is Jayden? That's all I need to know. It's the only reason I came here. You have already proven your loyalty, and that's fine. Jayden and I won't invite you to the wedding. I get it," I said.

Ava looked at me and exhaled a long breath. She leaned against the door and rolled her eyes.

"Bailey, this isn't gonna end well for you."

My cell phone rang. It was the detective on my case, which was the only reason I walked away. "Hello?"

"Miss Jones. We've found Michael. He's in custody in Mexico, and we've started the extradition process," the detective said.

I nearly skipped to my car as he poured over the latest information that would put Michael's thieving behind away for years.

"There's a personal call for you on Line One," Diane said. Her voice pulled me back to the present.

"Oh, who is it?" I asked. I blinked rapidly and tried to push the horrible memory completely out of my mind.

"She refused to say. Just said it was personal and she needed to talk to you about Jayden or something like that," Diane said.

I reached for the phone and thought, I can't take anymore!

CHAPTER FORTY-FOUR

Ava

I sat on the side of my bed and thought about all that had changed in my life. Bailey and I were no longer friends. She viewed me telling Sylvia about the affair as betrayal, and vowed to never forgive me.

Isaac was on the verge of moving out. I told him it was probably best that he go and be with Denise. For years, I looked at the poor choices Bailey made and thought my life was better since I was in a committed, monogamous relationship.

Boy, Sylvia and I talked about that poor chile like every incident was the next episode of *As the World Turns*. Who would've ever suspected that while we were busy critiquing everything she was doing wrong, we were both being made into fools?

When the door quietly opened, I turned my head and saw Sylvia.

"Hey, girl, want some company?"

I turned my torso and gave her a faint smile. "Come on in," I said.

"Look at us," Sylvia said, as she strode into my master bedroom. "Aren't we a hot mess?"

I nodded in acknowledgment.

"You don't know the half of it. How could we not have seen the signs? Both of our men were living double lives, and we were the very last to know," I said.

Sylvia eased onto the bed.

"What are you gonna do?"

I shrugged.

I looked around the room. This had been our sanctuary. The custom drapes that hung from the windows, the matching duvet, and throw pillows. The sitting room with the velvet chaise and the French doors that led to a small balcony—all of this was custom made to my taste. Several pictures of Isaac and me in happier times were spread around the room in black and silver frames.

"If you would've told me that my husband was screwing a younger woman, and going through the kind of drama he described, I would've looked at you like you had lost your mind," I said.

"Yeah. Well, at least your little homewrecker got the message. I can't believe Bailey's stupid behind actually thought she'd get the man." Sylvia leaned back on my bed, and looked up at the ceiling. "You know what, truth be told, she can have his old, tired ass!"

"That's what these young chicks don't get. Boo, if you really think he's upgrading, wait until he gets tired of you too," I said.

"Let's go get drunk! Hell, what's the point of sitting around here licking our wounds? It's not my concern what happens with Jayden when the dust settles, but your girl should know that he ain't with her ass, not because of me, though. That ain't where he wants to be," Sylvia said.

"You can say that again," I added. "You know what, the more I think about it, I don't feel up to going anywhere. I got wine, vodka, and Crown Royal. We can get drunk right here. If you're hungry, we can order in and chill. Besides, I'm not interested in catching a case behind these two poor excuses for husbands we got."

An hour later, when the doorbell chimed, I looked around and wondered whether Sylvia was downstairs.

"Ava, it's the pizza!" she yelled. "You coming down?"

"Yeah, just changing!"

We had several movies lined up. I mixed up a pitcher of Sour Apple Martini and we just needed the pizza and wings.

When I arrived downstairs, everything was set up and ready. I hadn't heard from Isaac most of the day and I was okay with that. Sylvia had been staying with me for the last week. She never said how long she'd be here and I didn't ask.

"Let's watch some comedy. Kevin Hart makes me laugh with his little, chocolate self," I said.

"Okay, let me put him on." Sylvia got up and started getting the show ready.

I refilled my drink and grabbed another slice of pizza and another wing.

"Girl. I think I should call it quits. I'm not scared to be alone. If Isaac wants a kid, and I can't give him one, he needs to go find someone who can." I stretched my legs across the chaise and sipped my drink.

"Why don't you guys get a surrogate? That Denise chick could've done it the right way from day one," Sylvia said.

I whipped my head in her direction.

"That's the thing. I'm not like Isaac. I don't feel like my life is incomplete because I didn't have any kids. The more I thought about it, I enjoyed our lifestyle the way it was. I enjoyed being able to pick up and go whenever the feeling hit me. I liked shopping for myself, and not having to think about what to get for kids. I really thought our marriage was strong when it was just him and me. Who knew the dirty, old bastard was feeling like he'd missed out on something since he didn't plant any seeds?"

Sylvia continued to chew her food. For a few moments, she didn't respond to what I had said. I wasn't sure whether she was thinking about my comments, or thinking about her own situation.

"I thought we were both on the same damn page! He never said he wanted kids, or even had a yearning," I muttered. When I felt the tears trying to push through, I stuffed my mouth with a wing.

"It's not about you, Ava. He's a man. They only think with that head between their legs. Girl, look at Jayden's simple behind. We are empty nesters. What the hell is he gonna go try and run around for? He can hardly keep it up longer than five damn minutes! How is that enough for anybody?"

I leaned forward.

"That's it, Sylvia. That's what the hell we're missing. There's someone out there willing to take anything just to say they have a man. Look at Bailey. She's gorgeous. Professionally, she's successful, but she can't hold on to a man. To her, it doesn't matter that he can't keep it up for more than five minutes."

Sylvia threw her head back and laughed.

I looked around. She started laughing harder. Soon, my girl was sounding like a hyena.

When Sylvia doubled over with laughter, I gave her a moment and waited.

"What's so funny?" I asked.

"It just dawned on me," she said as she struggled to regain her composure. "We've got those two nuccas by the balls! Dumb asses! Seriously. Name your price, whatever you want. You've heard that term, it's cheaper to keep her? Well, we 'bout to let them both know the true meaning of that."

I thought about what Sylvia was saying. And slowly, the idea took a hold of me. She had a damn good point. Why should we let them off the hook easy?

"Think about it, girl! We could drag the shit out for as long as possible, make them pay all the damn bills. Then, when they get tired, threaten to tie their asses up in court."

"Sylvia, I like the way you think!"

CHAPTER FORTY-FIVE

Jayden

I stood at the starting line with thousands of other runners who were participating in the Colorado Marathon. I checked my watch, adjusted my runner's cap, and shook out my legs and arms. When the gun fired, I moved forward towards the starting line and began the race. In many ways, it represented the start of my new life. Something I should have done long ago. I had moved to Denver after my divorce from Sylvia eighteen months ago. She got the house and a sizable portion of my retirement. I was able to get some of my retirement back through my portion of the equity that was in the house. Sylvia moved her mother in. Neither one of them enjoyed the idea of being alone. Since our divorce, my son has refused to talk to me. He's angry with me for hurting his mother so deeply, and I honestly don't blame him. Still, my heart is broken. I don't relish the idea that I destroyed what had become a family. Sylvia and I don't talk much, but when we do, I am happy that we're cordial. We did attempt to salvage our marriage through couple's counseling, but in the end, I found the courage and honesty to admit that I no longer wanted to be married. The counselor gave me some good advice to live by going forward. She said that a woman's heart is as tender as a man's balls. Don't break a woman's heart, and she won't bust your balls.

Bailey and I didn't work out for a number of reasons. After going through my divorce, I needed time to heal and to figure out what I wanted my life to look like. I had no desire to jump into a meaningful relationship with her. If I had, I would have only been repeating a pattern which would have led to hatred towards her. Bailey didn't like it when I pulled away from her, but eventually, she got the message that it was over. After I moved to Denver, I heard through the grapevine that she had gotten involved with another guy and the relationship went so sour that she suffered a breakdown, and had to be placed in a hospital. I don't know where she is now, but I hope she's healthy and happy.

Ava started the divorce proceedings with Isaac, but he talked her into going through marriage counseling before she made her final decision. As it turned out, Ava came to understand that by refusing to have children with Isaac, she had refused to meet his needs and accepted responsibility for her role in forcing him to seek fulfillment elsewhere. Once that was identified, they learned how to fully commit and communicate honestly, even if it hurt the other person temporarily. They found out how to speak each other's love language and to meet each other's needs. Ava stopped the divorce proceedings and gave their marriage another shot. Last I heard from Isaac, Ava was expecting and he could not be any happier.

As for me, I just continue to take life one step at a time. Now that I've had time to heal, mature, and rediscover myself, I am hopeful that I can find someone whom I can really love and be my true self with. I guess that's what life is partly about. Constantly growing and becoming more of who you're supposed to be, and finding someone who loves you for who you are, and not who they'd like you to be. Until I find that person, I'll just take every day one step at a time.

ABOUT THE AUTHORS

Pat Tucker's novel *Football Widows* is being made into a movie! By day, Pat Tucker works as a radio news director in Houston, Texas. By night, she is a talented writer with a knack for telling page-turning stories. A former TV news reporter, she draws on her background to craft stories readers will love. She is the author of seven novels and has participated in three anthologies, including *New York Times* bestselling author Zane's *Caramel Flava*. A graduate of San Jose State University, Pat is a member of the National and Houston Association of Black Journalists and Sigma Gamma Rho Sorority, Inc. She is married with two children.

Earl Sewell earned his Master of Fine Arts degree in Fiction Writing from Goddard College. Sewell has over twenty published works of fiction in various genres. His titles have enjoyed widespread success and have held steady positions on bestseller lists. He has been a guest lecturer at schools and universities around the country and has been featured in *The Washington Post, School Library Journal* and *Publishers Weekly*.